RECKLESS
HEARTS

A WICKED GAMES NOVEL

RECK LESS HEAR TS

a novel by
SEAN OLIN

KATHERINE TEGEN BOOKS
An Imprint of HarperCollins Publishers

Katherine Tegen Books is an imprint of HarperCollins Publishers.

Reckless Hearts
Copyright © 2015 by HarperCollins Publishers
All rights reserved. Printed in the United States of America.
No part of this book may be used or reproduced in any manner
whatsoever without written permission except in the case of brief quotations
embodied in critical articles and reviews. For information address
HarperCollins Children's Books, a division of HarperCollins Publishers,
195 Broadway, New York, NY 10007.
www.epicreads.com

Library of Congress Cataloging-in-Publication Data
Olin, Sean.
    Reckless hearts : a Wicked games novel / by Sean Olin. — First edition.
        pages   cm.
    Sequel to: Wicked games.
    Summary: Sensitive guitarist Jake has been trying to express his love
for his best friend, anime artist Elena, but when Elena connects online with
Harlow, sparking an instant connection, Jake is sure something is wrong but his
objections only push Elena into Harlow's arms.
    ISBN 978-0-06-219241-7 (hardback)
    [1. Best friends—Fiction.   2. Friendship—Fiction.   3. Dating (Social
customs)—Fiction.   4. Deception—Fiction.   5. Identity theft—Fiction.
6. Remarriage—Fiction.   7. Stepbrothers—Fiction.]   I. Title.
PZ7.O4682Rec   2015   2015005853
[Fic]—dc23   CIP
                                                                          AC

Typography by Carla Weise
15 16 17 18 19   PC/RRDH   10 9 8 7 6 5 4 3 2 1
❖
First Edition

1

DP Movers—their slogan was "You point the way, Dream Point!"—had arrived this morning at eight thirty. For the past three hours, they'd been carting boxes of clothes and books and kitchen utensils, and mostly, the carved figurines and masks and exotic musical instruments Jake Gordon's mother had collected from all over the world, into the flatbed of their truck and stacking them up in tight systematic rows. The moving truck, a pale cavernous brick of sea-foam aluminum, was almost full now. Almost ready to haul the history of Jake's life across town to the north shore, where the fancy people in Dream Point lived in their elaborate mansions, bunkered between their security gates and their private beaches.

Watching the movers sweat in the crisp December air, Jake had a hard time getting his head around the fact that he would be one of those fancy people now. He didn't feel like he'd changed at all, but his mother, Janey, had married Cameron Pendergrass, maybe the fanciest of them all. He owned the Mariana Hospitality Group, a chain of hotels all over the world, including three massive, full-service island resorts, one in the Bahamas, one in Antigua, and one on some island in the South China Sea. He was easily the richest person in Dream Point.

As the stringy tattooed guys who looked like they shouldn't be anywhere near this strong carried the last of the boxes from the house, Jake sat in a wicker-backed kitchen chair, its legs sinking into the moist soil of the front yard. He stared out at Greenvale Street and tried to distract himself from thinking how completely his life would change by wondering what would happen to all the stuff they were leaving behind. The couch, the dining room table, the bed he'd slept in since he was six years old, even the chair he was sitting in now—they were ditching all of it. The white stucco bungalow that Jake had always known as home—new people would be living in it by New Year's.

And Elena Rios, his best friend and partner in skeptical endurance of the cliquey, shallow life at Chris Columbus High, who knew all his secrets, or all but one—she'd no longer be living right next door. She'd promised to hang out with him and watch the movers work this morning, and he'd dragged two wicker-backed chairs out onto the lawn, but the one next to him was still empty.

He'd texted her three times already, giving her status updates on the movers' progress, and all he'd heard back was one hard-to-interpret message saying, "THESE THINGS TAKE TIME ;D." Tilted on the uneven soil of the lawn, the chair looked sad and lonely beside him.

"Hey, yo," the crew captain called to him from the back of the truck, squinting under the dingy red Santa hat he'd draped over his head. "You wanna sign off on this, or what?" He wagged a tin clipboard at Jake as though he thought Jake should have been able to read his mind.

Jake wandered over to the truck. His mother had put him in charge. She had to be at Tiki Tiki Java, the coffeehouse she owned on Shore Drive, and Cameron, obviously, wasn't interested in spending his precious time coordinating with moving companies—he had employees for that. School was out for Christmas break, so it wasn't like Jake had anywhere better to be, anyway.

"Just the boxes, yeah?" the mover said. "That's some nice stuff in there. You're leaving all of it?"

"Yeah," Jake said.

"The TV? That speaker system? Shit ain't cheap."

"Salvation Army is coming to take it away."

"Oh?" The guy raised an eyebrow. He was trying too hard not to seem overly curious. "When's that?"

"This afternoon," Jake lied.

The guy ticked his cheek. He braced the clipboard on his forearm and held the pen rubber-banded to it out to Jake. "You gotta push hard to get through all three layers," he said.

Jake signed the sheet and reminded the guy that his mother would be there to sign on the other side.

As the guy rounded up his three workers and closed the truck, Jake headed toward the house for one last look.

He checked his watch. It was almost noon. Still no sign of Elena.

She didn't usually flake like this, at least not with him. He knew she was elusive. She liked it that way. *Enjoy being with me while I'm here and don't ask for more.* That was her attitude. But Jake had always been the exception to this rule. He was the person she *didn't* hide from.

As he wandered the rooms of the house one last time, it took every ounce of his being to restrain himself from frantically bombarding Elena with the kind of needy, selfish where-are-you texts that he knew she hated getting from other people—her sister, her father, the couple of boys she'd briefly, disastrously dated.

He'd known her all his life. There was a photo of

the two of them in their diapers sitting in the dirt under the swing set in Seminole Park, reaching out to fumble at each other's chubby hands. She'd been there for him when his parents' marriage finally broke up and his father moved permanently to the Keys. He'd been there for her throughout the long saga of her mother's death of ovarian cancer and the roller coaster of chemo and radiation therapy, of hope and despair and hope and despair that had consumed her life for a year and a half. He'd watched her grow from a sassy, string-bean tomboy to a dark-haired, dark-eyed, darkly intelligent young woman whose sense of the world was as off-kilter as his own.

He adored her.

The truth was, he loved her.

He'd known it forever. Since middle school, at least, when they'd both begun to wonder why the other kids in their class seemed to always, only want to talk about LeBron James and Miley Cirus, when he'd begun to sense that Elena was the only person he knew who thought deeply about the world. She was curious, so curious that after she'd seen *Spirited Away*, the surreal, slightly spooky Miyazaki movie, she'd explored where it had come from and uncovered a whole world of Japanese anime. She didn't care if nobody else had heard of this stuff. It was interesting to her, and that was enough.

He loved that confidence he saw in her. He loved her compulsive joy, the goofy silliness she allowed herself to indulge in. And her fiery loyalty, the way she'd leap to the fight when she felt like he, or her sister, Nina, needed defending.

But it wasn't just that. Lately, it was physical, too. Her olive skin. Her perfect toes. The way she wore her hair in that modified pixie cut, close and tight around the back, her curls swooping up over her forehead. The sweet curve of her hips and the faint strawberry mark that peeked out like a tattoo from the side of her bikini bottoms.

If she weren't his best friend, he would have admitted it long ago. Even though he was just moving across town, he felt he had to tell her now. At least then she'd know that all those songs he'd written for "Sarah," the "girlfriend" who "lived down the beach from his dad in the Keys," had really been about her.

If only she'd come out to say good-bye, he could say the lines he'd been rehearsing all week.

He sent her one last text. "THEY'RE DONE. GOTTA GO IN 10."

She responded immediately. "LOOK OUT THE WIN-DOW."

And there she was in the chair he'd put out for her, casual, in tight jean shorts crisply folded up just above her knees, sporting her favorite *Cowboy Bebop* T-shirt. She made a goofy face, crossing her eyes and sticking out her tongue, briefly, then returned to hunching over the open laptop balanced on her thighs just in time to stop it from falling off.

The future—the future he'd imagined, anyway—flashed in front of Jake. Him moseying out of the house, hands in his pockets, playing it cool. Just as he reaches her, Elena looks up from the computer and something in her eyes says she knows what he's about to say. That wry grin of hers, capable of communicating both her relish in experience and her ironic commentary on how silly life can be, breaks over her face. And before he can even say, "It's always been you. I can't hide it anymore," she's up on her tiptoes, her arms stretched out around his neck. A kiss that releases the years of longing between them into the world.

He could almost feel it electrifying his cells already.

The slow walk out of the house was the easy part, even if he could feel his hands nervously shaking in his pockets.

"Hey," he said, from doorway.

"Hey is for horses," she said with a wink. And there was that grin, but it didn't convey the revelation of longing he'd imagined. "Sorry it took me so long." She patted the six-year-old MacBook that, through the strategic placement of black electrical tape, she'd made look like a monster chomping down on the Apple logo. "Technology. I had to reboot this sucker like five times this morning."

"Shaun White's not what he used to be, huh?" Jake said. Shaun White was the name Elena had given the computer.

"Shaun White should have retired years ago."

"Maybe I can ask Cameron to buy you an upgrade," Jake said. He meant it, though the idea of actually asking Cameron for anything made him nervous. He'd never spent any time around super-rich people and he wasn't sure he understood the codes they lived by.

Elena shot him a look that said, *Yeah right.* "I'd never let you put yourself in that situation." She focused on the screen for a second and tapped the touch pad a few times. "I mean, he didn't even come help you pack up."

"He's a busy guy."

"I know. I'm just saying," she said, protectively defending him.

Elena locked eyes with him for a second, and as her face softened and seemed to reach out to him, he knew she'd seen through to the part of him that was scared about all the change that moving into Cameron's mansion on the beach would create in his life.

"Come look at what I made you," she said.

Jake sat in the chair next to her, conscious of her body heat, not getting too close with his elbow or knee for fear of touching her—if he touched her, he'd melt.

"Come on, Jaybird," she said. "You have to be able to see the screen." And she threw her arm over his shoulder and mussed his hair, like a buddy, like she was about to give him a noogie. "You ready?"

She adjusted the volume and clicked play on her video-editing program.

First came the music. "You've Got a Friend in Me" from *Toy Story*. Then the delicate, slightly nervous script she always used in her animations.

For Jaybird, it said.

Jake immediately felt the emotions swell in his chest.

The animated characters that always represented the two of them in Elena's animes—Electra, the tough girl with spiky hair of black flames, heavy kohl eyes, padded, studded leather armor, and jet-flight platform shoes; and Jaybird, tall and skinny with knob knees and a constant bewildered expression on his face—performed a choreographed dance to the music. A backbeat kicked in, and Electra grew larger and larger, her mouth opening until the darkness inside swallowed up the screen.

As Elena's voice rap-talked over the *Toy Story* song, stylized freeze-frame images of the two of them floated in and out of the frame—highlights from their years of friendship: the day they raced their bikes all the way to the Seminole monument in the middle of town and then climbed triumphantly to the top and sat on the Native American warrior's back; the time Jake's mom took the two of them to Disney World and they spent the whole day pretending they weren't having as much fun as they really were; the moment when Jake played his guitar in front of an audience for the first time and Elena was right there clapping from the front row. Image after image of the two of them sharing each other's lives.

The song, or poem, or rap, or whatever Elena was calling the spoken word she'd layered over the images explained what was happening in them. She talked about the day her mom died and the long walk Jake had taken with her, not speaking at all, because what was there to do but be there, a presence by her side, ready when she needed him. She talked about the day he found out his parents were splitting up, how they'd snuck into the recycling center on the west side of town after dark and let out all their rage by shattering bottles against the wall, bottle after bottle after bottle after bottle, until they were giddy, until they'd almost forgotten how sucky the day had been.

"Most boys only want one thing," she said at one point. "But Jaybird's different. Jaybird sees the all of me."

The anime ended with another scrawled fragment of text. *Jaybird, don't you ever change!*

Jake was devastated. Not because he was sad but because he was so deeply touched by her work. He stared at the screen, frozen on the final image of the two of them holding hands, and he couldn't help but wonder if she'd be saying all these things if she knew how much he wanted to be more than friends with her.

"It's just a rough cut, but . . . what do you think?" she said, the look on her face betraying a real and desperate need to know he thought it was good.

"I love it," Jake said, trying to twist his lips into an earnest smile so she'd think he was telling the truth.

Her elegant eyebrows were arched in expectation, her whole face open, waiting.

"Should I post it to AnAmerica? You wouldn't mind?" AnAmerica was a web forum where Elena and other anime-obsessed kids from all over the country shared their animations with one another.

"Yeah. Yeah. Absolutely, you should post it. It's great."

But part of him was disappointed, too. No way could he confess his love to her now. Because what if she rejected him? What if she said, *Sorry, I love you, man, but I don't love you like* that? Better to be with her, even as friends, than to lose her friendship because he wanted more out of it than she did.

He rubbed his hands back and forth across his jeans, unsure what to do. "It's time," he said. He stood, dazed, and picked up his chair.

She flipped her lower lip down, trying to be cute as she made her sad face. When he didn't respond, she said, "Is everything okay?"

"Yeah. I've . . . I just have to lock up the house." He knew himself. He felt itchy. He had to get away. To go somewhere alone and lick his wounds. "And then I've got to go. I'm already late meeting Mom. Can you grab that chair?"

Leaving her computer on the lawn, she swung her chair above her head and carried it inside.

When it was time for them to say good-bye, he awkwardly held open his long arms for a hug. She fell into his chest, squeezing him tight, which was nice, but he couldn't bring himself to squeeze her back. He was afraid, if he did, that she'd see through him and learn his real feelings. Instead, he patted her chastely on the back.

"Don't forget us little people," she said.

"I won't. I'll see you soon," he said. "I'll call you every day. You'll see."

Even though Jake had said nothing would change, by that afternoon, it felt to Elena as though everything already had.

She was trapped at home—her least favorite place to be. Her sister, Nina, had closed the curtains tight across the half-moon living room window, shutting the house in darkness, and she sprawled in her crater on the plush yellow leather couch in front of the TV, shoveling Cool Ranch Doritos into her mouth. She didn't move once. She just lay there, watching episode after episode of *Storage Wars*, which she'd turned up so loud that Elena couldn't hear herself think, much less focus on editing the animation she'd made for Jake. She'd tried hunkering down in the kitchen. She'd tried locking herself in her bedroom. She'd even tried the bathroom, sitting on the floor with her computer propped on the closed lid of the toilet.

When, finally, Elena tried asking her sister to turn it down, Nina stared, her mouth open just enough to show her disinterest, and said, "I'm pregnant, Elena," as though that explained anything.

"And I'm trying to work," Elena responded. "I want to get this anime up on the site tonight."

Nina shrugged. "So do that, then," she said. She glared at Elena, challenging her to push the topic. "But I have to keep my feet up, so . . ." She jutted her chin out like she was putting a period on her statement.

Elena knew how this went. Her sister hadn't done much of anything but lie on the couch for the past month. She was overweight—by a lot—and being pregnant bloated her more. Her ankles had swelled when she'd hit her second trimester and her doctor had told her she needed to keep her feet elevated as much as possible. In the past month, Nina had done almost nothing but lie in her command center on the couch, her feet propped on one arm, her head lolling on the other. She wore the same pink Juicy Couture sweatsuit almost every day.

And what was Elena supposed to do? Argue with her? Tell her to get some exercise? Remind her that this was her house, too? She was pregnant! Being pregnant trumped everything.

"Fine," Elena said. She gave in, plopped on the tiled floor in front of the white fake Christmas tree draped in so much silver tinsel that the red balls hanging from it were barely visible, and watched the show with her sister.

Not five minutes later, Nina nudged her on the shoulder with a socked foot and said, "Can you get me a Diet Pepsi? Pretty please?" She smiled with a coy helplessness that was as annoying as the question.

"Nina! I'm not your maid," Elena said.

Nina rubbed her pregnant belly and readjusted the expression on her face to convey her helplessness with more conviction.

"Okay. But only if you turn it down."

As Nina made a show of playing with the volume buttons on the remote, Elena hopped off the floor and wiped the tinsel off the butt of her jean shorts. She padded around the couch and up the single step into the kitchen area. She grabbed a can from the fridge and faked throwing it at Nina's head before handing it to her.

"Should you really be drinking this while you're pregnant?" Elena asked.

"What's wrong with you today, anyway?" said Nina, defensively. "You're all pissy. If you want to do your thing, go over to Jake's house. You like it better there, anyway."

"You really don't know?"

Nina's face was blank.

"Today was the day. The movers came this morning."

"Oh!" said Nina. She reached out and squeezed Elena's shoulder, a quick massage, just enough to convey that she understood how sad this must make her.

"So I can't go over there."

"Tell you what," Nina said. "You take the controls. We'll watch what you want today."

Elena appreciated her sister's gestures toward sympathy and understanding. She knew Nina cared, in her lazy way. But her attempt to comfort her felt more like a burden than a gift. They were just so different. Elena had unending supplies of energy. She liked making stuff, using her imagination to explore her reality and transform it into extravagant cartoons. She liked the sunshine. She liked jangly music played live on the guitar, especially when she was near the ocean and there was maybe a campfire nearby. Her sister just sort of let her life happen to her.

More than anything else, it made her depressed. She hated the thought of being condemned to this house, wasting her life away in front of the TV, shutting down her brain and passively letting the world close in on her.

Of course, she couldn't tell her sister all this. Instead she said, "I don't care what we watch. Whatever you want. It's not like a different show will bring Jake back. Here—" She lobbed the controls back to her sister.

For the next three hours, they sat there, not moving, barely speaking, just staring at the obsessive freaks on the screen as they bid on box after box. Elena felt like a huge metal plate was being pressed down over her head, crushing her, pushing her into the floor. She felt both bored and trapped. She wondered how Nina could live like this all the time.

Then she wondered what was wrong with her that she was so ready to judge her sister—her pregnant sister! Life was just such a disappointment sometimes. Jake would understand how she felt. Jake would know how to make her feel better. But then, if Jake were around she probably wouldn't be feeling this way. She wouldn't even be here! She'd be outside somewhere with him, imagining, like they sometimes did, all the ways that, when Nina's baby was born, the two of them would make sure it had good taste, teaching it about art and music and culture.

Eventually, the familiar sound of her father jangling the spring-loaded clip on which he kept his keys broke the monotony. Elena could hear him futzing with the door before realizing it was already unlocked, and then there he was standing in the room with them, a look of exhaustion and smoldering frustration weighing down his face. His white guayabera shirt was stained with sweat at the armpits and his pleated linen pants had inched under his gut.

He flipped his keys back and forth around his finger,

slapping them repeatedly in the palm of his hand, taking in the situation at the house.

"*Hola*," he said. "Good to see you're all doing something constructive with your day."

With three great strides, he moved to the window and dramatically pulled the curtains open, filling the room with streaming evening sunlight. Elena and Nina shot quick wincing glances at each other, blinking in the suddenly bright light and bracing themselves for what was about to come. He was in a mood. *Everybody* was in a mood today.

"What's wrong with you?" Nina said bullishly.

He brushed his hand from the top of his bald head down over his bushy salt-and-pepper mustache, reigning in his thoughts. "What's wrong with me is, one, I've been zipping back and forth from one Super Suds to the other, dealing with all kinds of *mierda*—Selina locked her keys in her car on the south side and I had to open up for her, then the basement flooded on the west side . . . *uno, dos, tres, quatro*. Every single one of my Laundromats had something go wrong today. And then while I'm dealing with all this, what do I get? I get a call from a Mr. Ricardo Colon. You know that name? You should. That's Matty's parole officer—"

At the mention of her boyfriend's name, Nina shot up into a sitting position, ready to fight. "No, no, no, no," she said, waving her finger at her father. "I'm not his keeper."

"You see? Why don't you tell me why this Colon guy called me, hey?"

"I don't know," said Nina, defensively.

"Sure you do. Matty missed his appointment. Matty hasn't been to work. Matty this, Matty that. Matty's blowing it again." His voice rose a tick with each new item on his list. "Where is he? He heard me coming and snuck out the back door?"

"He's not here," said Nina.

"Oh? We must have run out of food, hey?" Elena's father shot back.

And then they were both shouting, rapidly, in Spanish. Elena was caught between the two of them, ducking as their words zipped back and forth above her head. She'd so had enough of this. All they ever did was fight, and always about Matty.

God, get me out of here, she thought. But where would she go? She couldn't flee to Jake. It's not like she could ride her bike all the way across town and show up at *Cameron Pendergrass's* estate, begging to be let in. He'd think, *Who's this crazy Cuban girl and why's she on my lawn?*

Her dad was stalking around the room now, circling Nina. And Nina was wagging her finger all over the place. Elena couldn't take it anymore.

"Everybody! Shut up for a second!" she said. She leaped to her feet, putting herself physically between them. Turning to them one at a time, she said, "Dad. Matty hasn't been here all day. I've been sitting right here. I would have seen him. And Nina. Dad's right. You have to get Matty under control. What are you going to do when the baby is born and he disappears for days on end, or shows up drunk in the middle of the night shouting for you to come out and party with him? He's the father of your child. Tell him to get it together. Jeez."

She didn't usually get involved in their fights like this, and the two of them stared at her in surprise for a beat. Then they turned right back to each other and commenced shouting again.

"You people are hopeless!" Elena said.

But neither of them even heard her. They didn't notice when she slinked out of the room, either. They just kept on yelling. It was almost like they *liked* the drama.

She padded down the hall to her room, feeling with each step how wrong it was to head in this direction, farther into the house, when she should have been moving in the other direction, out into the crisp night air, toward Jake's place next door, where they'd find a way to remind each other that laughing about their troubles always made things better. But she couldn't do that. For the first time since Jake had driven away with his guitar and the duffel bag of clothes in the backseat of his beat-up old Jeep, which they affectionately called the Rumbler, Elena sadly understood how her life would be different without him living next door.

Locking the dead bolt she'd placed on her door, she sparked up her computer, put on her headphones, and checked out the new animations her virtual friends had posted on AnAmerica, hoping they'd be distracting enough to drown out the drama on the other side of the door.

3

Jake had never seen a house quite like this one. It was like something out of a magazine. It had been featured in a magazine, actually. *Luxury*, it was called. Jake had never heard of it, but the name said everything he needed to know. It was hidden from the street by a solid white gate and the first time Jake had seen the surreally lush lawn he'd wondered how many thousands of dollars Cameron spent every month on landscaping. There were no trees, just this vast flat green space perched above the beach and the house sitting there like a sculpture.

From the outside it looked like a set of blindingly white boxes, each one set off-center from the ones above and below it, like children's blocks that had been placed precariously on top of one another. Inside, it was a cavernous, flowing open space with different platformed levels connected by brushed concrete stairs that seemed to float free in the air.

The interior was so tasteful that there weren't any Christmas decorations, not even a wreath. Jake felt like he was in an art gallery, not someplace people lived. But people did live here. He lived here now. It would take some getting used to.

That first night, as he sat at the hand-carved, blond-wood dining table—positioned in just the right off-angle location in the big oblong main room that was, all by itself, larger than his old house across town—he had the strange feeling that he and his mother and Cameron were guests at a five-star restaurant that only served one party a night.

They were served by a waiter with artfully mussed hair and a carefully untucked linen shirt, which he wore over crisp jeans and white no-brand sneakers. He looked casual but brought their duck confit and shaved fennel salad to the table with regimented efficiency. Jake wished Elena were here to see it—he could imagine the arched eyebrow she'd throw his way, the way she'd poke him under the table and slowly twist her silver custard spoon in the air, studying it like a mystifying artifact from an alien civilization until she finally got Jake to chuckle over the pomposity that was surrounding him.

Cameron didn't seem to notice the waiter was even there. He held court, telling stories about the various adventures he'd had over the years, most of them involving the yacht he owned and small islands in the Caribbean. He was a small guy with big hair, a smaller guy than he seemed like he should be, given how much space he took up. He was the kind of man who never buttoned the top two buttons of his shirt, even when he wore a suit. Throughout the meal, he'd been leaning all over his seat and sprawling into the empty chair next to him, stretching his arms and legs out like he was inviting everyone to take their shoes off and chill.

"So, we looked out from the top of the cliff and Wickman points toward the bay and says, 'Hey, check it out. Someone's boat is floating away,'" Cameron was saying now. "And I look, and holy fuck. It's *my* boat!"

Jake could tell his mom was in awe of him, that this new life she'd pulled Jake into was a kind of fantasy to her, a life of stylish leisure that she'd always dreamed of. The way she gazed at him, her chin on her hand, barely blinking her big blue eyes—it was like she was disappearing into his aura. Cameron hardly noticed how starstruck she was. He seemed to assume that women would respond to him this way.

"It was drifting sideways, a good hundred yards out already. The bay was so deep that the anchor hadn't reached the bottom. So we had no choice, we had to dive. Operation Save the Boat. My first foray into extreme sports."

Pouring with one hand while gesticulating and illustrating his story with the other, he almost unnoticeably kept Jake's mom's wineglass full of pinot gris.

Jake quietly took it all in, trying to make sense of his new reality. His mom's romance with Cameron Pendergrass had been a whirlwind of frantic change. She'd met him only four months ago, when he'd hired Tiki Tiki Java to cater a reception at StarFish, the glitzy hotel he owned in Dream Point. Jake had barely met the guy before they'd suddenly gotten engaged and then, two weeks later, married, in a secret ceremony that not even Jake had been invited to on that yacht somewhere off the coast of St. John. He was happy for his mom, of course. She'd been lonely for a long, long time. But he was baffled by how to relate to Cameron. The guy intimidated him.

"You want a pour?" Cameron asked Jake, pointing the half-empty wine bottle at Jake's glass.

Jake glanced at his mother, who subtly shook her head no. "No thank you, sir," he said.

"It's Cameron to you, Jake. We're family now."

A voice from the other side of the room called out, "I'll have a glass. Since you're offering."

Everyone turned to see a guy Jake's age leaning against the wall near the front door to the house like he'd been there for a while, watching them. He was tall, though not as tall as Jake, and fit under his formfitting rich-navy-blue T-shirt in a metrosexual way. He had stylishly cut blond hair and was wearing sunglasses that must have cost as much as Jake's car.

The way Jake's mom lightly touched Cameron's hand, as though to brace him and calm his nerves, made Jake think that the guy wasn't welcome. He wondered who he was and how he'd gotten here.

"Glad you could make it," Cameron said. "You're only, oh"—he made a show of checking his Omega watch—"two hours late."

When the guy smirked it was like he was flashing a switchblade. "Well, you know, anything for you, Cameron," he said. "How 'bout that wine?"

He sauntered toward the table like he owned the place and the waiter appeared out of nowhere to silently set a fourth place setting at the table.

As Cameron grudgingly poured a dollop of wine into the glass that had appeared with the new place setting, Jake caught his mother's eye and mouthed, *Who's that?*

She cleared her throat. "Jake, this is Nathaniel. Cameron's son. He's in town from the Roderick School in Atlanta. Nathaniel, this is my son, Jake."

With a flourish, Nathaniel reached out his hand to shake. "How are you," he said, and then after a pause he added, "brother."

His grip was a vise, like he'd been told by someone—Jake couldn't imagine it would have been laid-back Cameron—that a firm handshake was the key to success in the world and he'd turned this wisdom into a competitive dare.

"Sorry I'm late," he said, glancing at his father. "I had, you know, other things to do."

Cameron patted him on the back, shot him a sharp glance, and said, "You'll do better next time."

Jake's mom chimed in. She'd always been good at playing the gracious hostess. "We're just glad you could make it at all," she said. "It means a lot to your father. And I can say, for me, I've been dying to meet you since he first mentioned you."

"Oh," Nathaniel said drolly, "he mentioned me?"

"Of course he did. He loves you, Nathaniel." She gave Cameron's hand one last pat and then withdrew her own hand back into her lap.

Nathaniel grinned at this, showing off his sharp white teeth, and seeming, briefly, touched by what he'd heard. "Aww. Shucks," he said.

The tension between Cameron and Nathaniel was overpowering. Jake could sense it in the way Cameron subtly adjusted his posture to make more room between himself and his son. He could feel it in the sharp end to Nathaniel's charm, the way he was displaying his refusal to defer to his father.

He again wished Elena could be here to see this. He tried to imagine her making one of her silly faces at him, secretly letting him know she was noticing the same weirdness he was and reminding him simply by sticking out her tongue that he shouldn't take it too seriously.

"Now—" Nathaniel took a swig of wine, downing the small amount his father had allowed him in one swallow. "That cliff. It was a hundred-foot sheer drop. The water was so clear that you could see the floor. I have this right, Cameron? Should I tell them how it ends? They survived. They saved the boat. That's Cameron for you. He'll do anything to save that boat." He raised his empty glass and said, "But cheers to that, hey?"

Cameron met his challenge and graciously, indulgently, touched glasses with him. "Cheers to that," he said.

Jake got the sense that Cameron could squash Nathaniel any time he wanted and it was just his good heart that stopped him from doing so. He wondered what had brought the two of them to this point, and how long their antagonism had persisted. Nathaniel's behavior didn't seem like the usual teenaged rebellion.

It felt uncomfortable just being in the room with them. There was a story here, a lifetime of resentments and secrets that Jake might never know. If Elena were here, she'd be taking mental notes so they could go over it all together later, dreaming up explanations filled with dangerous intrigue. But she wasn't here. And even though she was just a couple miles across town, she seemed farther away than she ever had. It struck him that this was the first time in forever that he'd have spent an evening away from her.

4

Even with her headphones on and the volume turned up as high as it would go, Elena could hear her father and sister going at it on the other side of her locked bedroom door.

Sitting at the drafting table she used as a desk, she tried to ignore them, to fill her headspace up with the new clips her friends on AnAmerica had uploaded. There was a spoof of *Hello Kitty* by EvilTwin82 in which the cute pillowy cat was mutilated into a cartoonish sea of blood. There was an amusing journey through the daily life of an ant by NaNo_NoLa. An abstract dance of colored lights choreographed to a Yo-Yo Ma song by CelloMello. Another installment in the ongoing saga of

"The 98-Pound Weakling" by ImNotNervous. But none of them held her attention the way she needed. None of them could compete with the never-ending soap opera of her family.

They were arguing over the remote now. Her dad was saying something about the Heat, how there was a crucial game against the Pacers tonight and no way was he going to let Nina stop him from watching it, even if she *was* pregnant. Elena didn't even want to know.

She watched a clip of a crime-fighting dog and cat who solved their cases, usually involving evil squirrels, by accident as they chased each other around the neighborhood. She liked this one. FranSolo was the name of the girl who'd created it. Elena wrote a comment on her page. "I always knew those squirrels were up to no good!"

Having run out of clips to watch, she got down to work uploading her new animation—the one she'd made for Jake—to the site.

Electra, her online tag, was a kind of celebrity on AnAmerica, and she knew a lot of love would be coming her way soon. With nothing better to do with herself, she sat back and stared at the screen, waiting for the outpouring of likes and comments to rack up under her new clip.

And here they came. One, two, three, fifteen, twenty, twenty-five likes. It felt good to see them every time, though she didn't know why—it's not like they really meant anything. The comments started rolling in.

"*Toy Story* is the best movie ever!"

"So sorry to hear Jaybird is moving away!"

"Very cool, Electra!"

As usual, everyone was so nice to her here. So why did she still feel so empty inside? Stupid question. She knew why.

The sound of the basketball game blasted from the TV in the other room. And her father's voice: "So go somewhere else, Nina. It's not like you forgot how to walk when you got pregnant."

She whipped out her phone and shot a text to Jake. "YOUR VIDEO IS LIVE." Then she immediately sent him another one. "I MISS YOU!"

His response came within seconds. "I MISS YOU TOO! RICH PEOPLE ARE WEIRD!"

For the first time all evening she felt in some small way connected to the world.

5

Jake had trained himself to know when a new song was coming on. He could feel the rhythm in the fingers on his strumming hand. He'd unconsciously start miming out the chords and catching strings of lyrics in his mind. He'd learned to take note of these phenomena, to mark them and memorize them and hold them tight until he could begin doodling around them and teasing them into a musical form. Or better, to drop what he was doing immediately and follow the music wherever it was leading.

And tonight, after that uncomfortable dinner, he'd caught sight of the night view of the ocean from his new bedroom window for the first time—all that endless black water beyond the gray moonlit dunes—and known a sweet and slightly sad new melody was beginning to form in him.

Sitting on an unpacked box, surrounded by stacks of other unpacked boxes, he strummed at his favorite guitar, a worn old Gibson his father had given him way back when he was twelve, and tested various chord progressions. He had two phrases in his head—*everything a boy could want, everything but you* and *don't let the sea wash me away.* He knew they went together but he hadn't figured out exactly how.

He gazed out the window again and studied the way the blackness of the sky met the even darker blackness of the water. A new line came to him. *I carved your name in the sand with a stick.* Maybe it could be the first line. He tested the line out, fingerpicking in a slow minor key beneath it.

To inspire himself, he'd propped his computer on one of the stacks of boxes and pulled up Elena's AnAmerica page. Her talent, and the energy she put into developing it, always inspired him. He had a notion that this song could be a response to the beautiful video she'd made for him, though he still wasn't sure if he'd admit this to her. For now, it might be better to continue pretending he was pining for "Sarah," the free-spirited Key West beach bunny he'd invented to explain to her where all his love songs were coming from.

A new fragment came to him as he stared at her page: *don't hate me for loving you*. He knew this one would find its way into the song. It was the most honest line so far. It described what was going on inside him exactly.

Don't hate me for loving you
Oh-o'delay
Don't let the sea wash me away

Maybe that could be the chorus. It was a start.

He sang the lines again and again, changing his intonation and phrasing in little ways, running through the possible variations in search of the perfect version.

When he looked up from his guitar again, he was startled to see Nathaniel sitting on the sleek Scandanavian dresser across the room, slouching against the wall, smirking at him. His feet dangled off the edge and he tapped the drawers rhythmically with the heel of his polished black shoe. He seemed nervous, like there was a bundle of energy trapped inside him, bucking against his skin, trying to get out.

"Not bad," he said. "Where'd you learn to pick like that?"

Jake clutched his guitar as though he could hide the music he'd been making. He didn't like being distracted when he was composing. But like everything else about this foreign house, the bedroom didn't feel like it belonged to him enough for him to tell Nathaniel to leave.

"I . . . My dad's a musician," he said. "He taught me."

"Oh yeah?" said Nathaniel. "Have I heard of him?"

In his right hand, Nathaniel held an ornately decorated silver flask that had been inlaid with an image of a stalking tiger, delicately carved in ivory. He raised it to his lips and poured a nip of whatever it contained into his mouth as he waited for Jake to respond.

"He used to be in a band. Hope Springs. Kind of folky-bluesy stuff. They had a song called 'Dandelions.' You might have heard that one."

"That song was huge. That guy's your dad?"

"It wasn't that huge. Nobody got rich off it. It went to number eighty-six."

Jake glanced at his guitar, wishing he could get back to work.

"Still . . ." Nathaniel warbled a few lines of the chorus to Jake's dad's minor claim to fame. Then, tipping the flask toward Jake, he said, "Want some forty-year-old, oak-cask rum?"

Jake shook his head no, but then realizing that since Nathaniel showed no signs of leaving, he wouldn't be getting any more work done on the song, he changed his mind. He felt like he should probably get to know his new stepbrother, anyway. "Know what, sure," he said.

Popping down from the dresser, Nathaniel handed Jake the flask. The ivory inlay was impossibly intricate. It depicted some sort of Chinese landscape complete with mountaintop and weeping trees and a wise old man with a cane climbing a lonely path.

"How do you like the room?" Nathaniel asked, wandering around and poking his nose in the various boxes Jake had opened but not unpacked.

"It's okay, I gu—"

Cutting him off, Nathaniel went on. "It used to be mine. That dresser? Mine. That bed? Mine. That bookshelf? Mine. I guess what's mine is yours now, though, brother. Enjoy it."

This was news to Jake. "They gave me *your* room?" he said, wincing at the burn as the rum hit his throat.

He felt a tug of guilt over having taken Nathaniel's room, though Nathaniel didn't seem all that upset about it. He just kept on poking around in the boxes, lifting things out to study them and then putting them back.

"Fuck it. That's what happens when you don't come home for two years."

Every new detail Jake learned about this guy led to a hundred more questions. "Two years. Wow. That's a long time. You didn't come home once?"

Nathaniel threw him a look as if to say, *Isn't it obvious?* "You'll see," he said. "Once you know Cameron like I do, you won't be asking questions like that." He

37

peered at the screen of Jake's computer. "Who's this?"

Jake blushed. He felt exposed, like just having Elena's profile open like this was a betrayal of the secrets of his heart. Instead of answering, he said, "Did something happen between the two of you?"

"You're hilarious," Nathaniel said. He took the flask back and downed a large shot of rum. "He's my father. Is that not enough?" He went back to studying Elena's profile. "Electra. And that makes you Jaybird."

Jake could tell that he shouldn't push the topic too hard, but he had to ask. "Why aren't there any photos of you anywhere? I mean, I didn't even know you existed. That's sort of weird."

"Ask Cameron, not me." Nathaniel pulled up a box and sat in front of Jake. "Let's talk about Electra. She's obviously much more interesting to you than the ongoing saga of Nathaniel and Cameron. That song you're writing for her is pretty sweet. But eventually you're going to have to come clean with her."

Just the thought of telling Elena how he felt made Jake's heart swell until it almost cracked in half. Immediately defensive, he said, "She's my friend, that's all."

"She's your friend whose pants you want to get into. Unless you're lying to yourself, too." Taking another nip from his flask, Nathaniel stared at Jake like he was trying to break him. "I don't think that's true, though. 'Don't hate me for loving you'? You know exactly how you feel."

Jake didn't know what to say. Nathaniel was right, of course, but he didn't seem to understand how sensitive and complicated the situation was.

"I know how it goes, man. I've been there," Nathaniel said.

"Have you?" Jake said shyly.

Nathaniel smirked knowingly. "Here's the thing." He handed Jake the flask again. "Drink up." As Jake forced himself to swallow down a little bit more of the rum, Nathaniel laid it out for him. "You can go on following her around forever, making puppy-dog eyes, knotting yourself up inside, dying a little bit every time she mentions some other guy, but you'll never get what you want that way. You've gotta make your move. That's the only play."

Maybe it was the rum or maybe it was the fact that they were in this intimate space that had once been Nathaniel's and was now Jake's, or maybe it was just that Nathaniel seemed so much more self-confident and successful at life than Jake, but Jake felt like he could trust him, like he had something to learn from his new stepbrother. "If I never make a move, she can never reject me," he said, admitting his deepest fear.

"So let her reject you. Then get on with your life," Nathaniel said. "There's a lot of fish in the sea."

Jake knew he was right, but that didn't make the truth hurt any less. He nervously picked out the few bars he'd written of his new song.

"There you go," Nathaniel said. "Sing your heart song. And stick with me. I won't steer you wrong, brother."

6

By the next day, Elena's new Jake-less reality had begun to sink in. She sat on the tile floor in the living room, cradled in a misshapen pink-and-yellow polka-dot chair pillow that just barely fit in the space next to the tree, tooling around on her computer to distract herself from her sister's television program and, hopefully, escape the funk she'd fallen into since Jake had moved away.

The show today was *Hoarders*—even worse than *Storage Wars*.

As Elena bounced back and forth among BuzzFeed and Twitter and her own AnAmerica page, which was still racking up likes and comments now, three days after she'd posted her latest animation, she couldn't help but track the gist of what was happening on the show. A woman in her forties who rescued cats to comfort herself from all the ways she couldn't rescue herself is confronted by her worried parents after they discover that the house she lives in is so overrun that she's now sleeping in her garage.

The thought that Elena was supposed to find this entertaining disgusted her, but she wasn't about to say anything to her sister. Nina loved it. She sucked on a giant candy cane and periodically popped it out of her mouth to click her tongue at the outrages the show paraded across the screen, shaking her head, bugging her eyes at Elena.

"Ay-yi-yi-yi!" she said.

Elena smiled in recognition and checked her AnAmerica page. A new comment popped up. Some guy going by the handle Harlow. "You're the best artist on this site," he said.

A grin broke across her face. She didn't get compliments like this all the time, and it felt good to be singled out. She wondered who this Harlow guy was.

"Flattery will get you everywhere," she said.

"Love the way you reference those seventies posters of big-eyed children."

She was surprised to see that he had caught the reference. She hadn't realized that anyone but her even knew those posters existed. Commenting back, she said, "Big-eyed kids. Good catch. So sad and yet so sweet. Thanks for the shout-out."

"These people!" said Nina, gawking at the TV. "How do they live with themselves?"

Elena didn't know where to begin answering this question. She looked at the nest of cast-off clothing Nina had strewn around herself, the glass-topped coffee table Nina had crammed with food like a buffet table from hell: takeout tacos, three more candy canes, Diet Pepsi, Cheez-Its, and the pineapple she'd been craving nonstop lately. Elena could see the seeds of a *Hoarders* episode taking root right here in her own house.

She wanted to say, *Nina, look at yourself before you start judging other people. Think about what you're doing to your unborn child.* But this was just too mean. She knew that her sister was in real discomfort today. She'd thrown up all morning. Her ankles were so swollen that she couldn't even fit socks over them. Feeling bad for her, Elena had made a promise to herself to be cheerful and kind and to baby Nina today in the way she knew nobody else would. Trying to play along with her sister's mood, she said, "It's good that she's getting help. The producers are going to give her a whole new house. I just worry about what will happen to all those cats."

"The cats!" Nina said. "It's just too much!"

"Mmm," Elena said as she scanned an article about

Scarlett Johansson on Flavorwire. She tabbed back to AnAmerica to see if Harlow had responded to her comment yet. He had.

"They remind me of the graffiti I saw last time I was in Paris. Big-eyed kids are making a comeback there."

"I'll take your word for it. I've never been to Paris," she wrote.

"We can change that," he responded.

This made her smirk. "Oh yeah? How are we going to do that?"

"We'll take my private jet."

She smirked again. This Harlow guy was fun. But he couldn't possibly have a private jet, right?

Before she could respond he shot her another message. "JK." Then another one. "Who's the emo boy?"

"Jaybird?"

"Yeah."

"A friend."

"Boyfriend?" he asked.

Elena knew he was fishing. Before answering, she pulled up his user profile in a separate screen and scanned it for signs that he might be a creep. There wasn't a lot there. His profile picture was an aerodynamic cartoon motorcycle with giant jet boosters flaring out the back. Under likes, he'd listed "*Cowboy Bebop*, Studio Ghibli, getting lost in foreign cities where I don't know the language," and, mysteriously, "trouble." She decided to risk it. She hadn't flirted with anyone in a long time.

"No. Just a friend," she wrote.

His response came immediately. "So let's go to Paris."

"We've already covered this," she said.

"Right. How 'bout this. I'll bring Paris to you."

She couldn't help but smile at this.

Her sister poked her with a toe. "Elena, you're missing the best part," she said. "What's so funny, anyway?"

"Nothing, just . . . internet stuff."

Elena glanced at the television. The shrink and the camera crew were wandering through the cat lady's house, poking at the six-foot-high stacks of empty litter containers, saying how nauseating the place smelled. "This is the good part?" she asked her sister.

Grinning, Nina shoveled a handful of Cheez-Its into her mouth. "Uh-huh," she said, dribbling crumbs onto her sweatshirt.

Elena shrank a little bit inside. This family. These people. How had she ever come to be related to them?

When she jumped back to the chat screen, she saw that Harlow had left a new message. "Still there?"

She typed quickly. "Yeah. Sorry. My sister's annoying me."

"Why?"

Where to start? She wasn't sure she wanted to subject this stranger to the craziness of her family struggles just yet, but she knew better than to let the conversation go much further on the public comments board. She suggested they take the conversation into private mode.

"So? Your sister?" he asked, when they'd switched over.

Elena could feel herself chickening out. She didn't know this guy well enough to go into the gory details of Nina's troubles. Instead, she said, "Do you ever want to just run as far away as you can get from everything?"

"Every minute of every day," he said.

"How do you deal with it?"

"I get on my motorcycle and just go, go, go. One day I'll go and never come back."

"I want to do that," Elena said.

"What's stopping you?"

"I don't have a motorcycle."

"I can solve that," he said, adding a winking emoticon.

"Just like you can fly me to Paris on your private jet."

"LOL. I really do have a motorcycle."

She took a closer look at his profile. His location was listed as South Florida, which gave Elena a little thrill. There was no harm in idly dreaming that this witty guy who admired her art and knew how to flirt online might be perfect for her. No harm in imagining that he'd been hiding right under her nose all this time.

Then in a new message, she said, "So your profile says you like trouble."

"Yeah."

"What kind of trouble?"

"As Marlon Brando said, 'Whadda ya got?'"

This actually made her laugh out loud. She was brought back to earth when she glanced at Nina and saw her struggling to sit up on the couch and hobble on her swollen feet toward the bathroom.

See, this, this was why she couldn't run away. Her sister, her father, everyone needed her to be the sane and capable one around here. She didn't want to turn the TV on one day and see them on an episode of *Hoarders* or *Intervention*, or what was the other one? *Cops*.

"Gotta go. Nice chatting," she typed, quickly shutting the computer.

Then, hopping up, she scrambled after her sister. "Nina, wait," she called. "Let me help you."

7

"Sounding good, brother."

Nathaniel was back, leaning against the sliding door that opened out from the cavernous living area onto the massive porch where Jake had been practicing his new song. He'd just taken a midafternoon shower and was wrapped in one of the impossibly plush, massively large towels with which the house was stocked.

Annoyed by the intrusion, Jake looked up from his guitar and stopped playing. "Thanks," he said, propping his bare foot on the rail of the porch and slouching back in the chair he'd dragged over.

He had a gig tonight at Tiki Tiki Java, his standing Thursday-night show, but this one was different because he'd made up his mind to play the new song for Elena. It was finished now. His most honest song ever. There was no way she'd be able to hear it and not know it was about her.

"You got a title yet?" Nathaniel asked.

"I think I'm going to call it 'Driftwood.'"

Jake strummed a couple chords, hoping Nathaniel would get the hint and go away. He didn't want to be rude. He picked out a timid melody. The guy wouldn't leave. He was just about to get up and go somewhere else himself when he heard the telltale buzz of a bee zipping around his head.

He froze, momentarily terrified.

Having lived with his allergy for so long, he didn't even have to think about how to react. He just listened and tried not to move a muscle.

Out of the corner of his eye, he could see Nathaniel cocking his head and studying him with a look on his face that said he found what was happening cruelly amusing.

"You okay?" Nathaniel said.

The buzz tracked closer to Jake's head and he dug his chin into his neck, trying to avoid but not incite it.

"I'm allergic to bees," he explained.

Nathaniel chuckled. "It's always something, right?" he said. "No worries. I've got you covered." For a moment, he tracked the bee, following it with his nose. Then he clapped his hands together and the buzzing stopped and the bee fell to the porch railing, dead.

Jake exhaled. "Thanks," he said. But he couldn't help feeling like there was something aggressive, some sort of power play, in the way Nathaniel had nonchalantly taken care of the bee for him.

"Not a problem." Nate flicked his finger and sent the bee out into the dunes. He leaned against the railing and folded one leg over the other. "Electra gonna be there tonight?" he asked. "What am I saying? Of course she is. Look at you."

Jake had put on his best pair of jeans. He'd rummaged through his T-shirt drawer until he'd found the iron-on *Speed Racer* shirt she'd gotten him for Christmas last year. A special outfit, yes, but how would Nathaniel have known?

"What do you mean by that?" he asked Nathaniel. "Do I look anxious or something?"

Nathaniel made that face of his, the one that might mean he was judging you or might mean he was just being smugly friendly. "Do you look anxious?" he said. "You look like you're halfway to a heart attack. You gonna make your move?"

"I'll see how it goes," Jake said vaguely, trying not to give anything away. He gazed out at the ocean and let the breeze smother his face.

"Dude. Confidence," Nathaniel said. He was tapping his thumb against his pec in a weird way that seemed both casual and rehearsed. "You've got a few things to learn about girls, don't you?"

"What's that supposed to mean?" The last thing Jake wanted right now was unsolicited advice from Nathaniel. Every interaction they'd had since that first night in Jake's room had felt tinged with undercurrents of competitive malice. Jake didn't take it personally. It seemed more of a function of Nathaniel's personality than anything specifically directed at Jake, but he'd begun to suspect that the two of them would never be the friends that Nathaniel seemed to want them to be.

"I'm just saying, you're a nice guy," Nathaniel said, pulling a chair up next to Jake's. "Nice guys don't win."

"I'm not trying to win."

"See, that's where you're wrong." Nathaniel pulled a pack of Marlboro Lights out of the waist of his towel and flipped it open. "You *do* want to win. You want to win Electra's undying devotion." He tapped out a lighter and a cigarette. "You want her to lie in bed aching for you. You want to see her and be able to tell that she's drowning inside her desire for you. If that's not winning, I don't know what is. And I'm telling you, it's never gonna happen as long as you keep trying to be a nice guy."

Jake just stared at him. He felt trapped and suffocated

by this conversation and he couldn't figure out how he'd fallen into it. "You've got to be kidding me," he finally said.

Nathaniel shrouded his cigarette from the wind and lit it.

"Listen," he said, leaning in conspiratorially. "Cameron's an asshole. We've already established that. But a shrewd kind of asshole. He knows what he's doing. And, brother, that dude gets more pussy than anybody I've ever met."

Jake wasn't sure how to take Nathaniel's attitude toward Cameron. First that Nathaniel would talk this way about his own father. Then that he might be telling the truth. It couldn't be true. Jake's mother would never marry a guy like that.

Nathaniel leered at him. "The one helpful thing he's ever taught me—girls want the bad boy. They want the guy who doesn't care about them. They want to pine and fret over whether you love them. That's just the facts, Jack. Make her think she's got to beg and grovel for your devotion and she'll give you whatever you want."

Jake retreated into picking at his guitar. He was repelled by the thought that Nathaniel would want him to aspire to this sort of behavior. Jake had seen guys like this who, as Nathaniel had said, got whatever they wanted. There was a guy nicknamed Rollo, a thick-necked wrestler who'd graduated from Chris Columbus a couple years ago and who'd been a total bastard toward women who always seemed to be falling all over him. Elena used to rant about him all the time. His name— Rollo—had become a secret code between them, a word they used to refer to guys like that in general.

"Elena's not like that," he told Nathaniel. "She's enlightened."

"That's what you think," Nathaniel said. "They're all enlightened. Until they're not."

Jake wanted to punch him. He felt his muscles clenching.

"Now I've hit a nerve. Sorry, brother. Just trying to help."

But Nathaniel didn't seem all that sorry. He leaned over the rail and flicked the end of his cigarette out into the dunes. Then he flashed that look of his again and patted Jake on the shoulder.

"Let me know how it goes."

He adjusted his towel and wandered back into the house, and when Jake began practicing his song again he found that he couldn't concentrate. All he could think about was Elena swooning and fawning over an asshole like Rollo. Something like that would never happen, he told himself, but now that Nathaniel had placed the idea in his head, he couldn't get it out.

8

When she arrived at Tiki Tiki Java, Elena was so excited to see Jake that she threw herself off her bike, leaving it to spin its wheels on the patch of lawn out front as she raced through the bamboo-covered outside seating area that had been strung with white Christmas lights into the main room of the café. Jake's mom had really done the place up for the season. Spray-on snow frosted the windows and intricate snowflakes had been stenciled onto the glass. A massive Christmas tree sat in one corner of the room, festooned with ornaments fitting for a café that took pride in its tropical location: plastic pineapples and bananas, a surfing Santa, reindeer in sunglasses.

Elena hardly saw the mothers with strollers and old fogeys reading their newspapers and the few hipper, looser, younger people who'd begun to show up for Jake's gig—her eyes were focused on Jake, seated, as she knew he would be, at the small round table next to the platform where he would perform. It had been only three days since they'd seen each other, but it felt like a lifetime.

He gazed up at her with his shy smile and she was pleased to see that he looked just like himself, so tall that he seemed folded into his seat, his light brown hair mussed and a little too long, like an overgrown little boy. He'd worn the faded *Speed Racer* shirt she'd bought him last year for Christmas and on the table in front of him was a pink smoothie, which she knew must be for her, since he'd never let that kind of sugary, milky drink gum up his throat before he had to sing.

"Hey-o!" she said, sliding into the seat across from him. "Jake. Jaybird. Where've you been my whole life?"

He blinked at her with his wide, pale eyes. "Your smoothie, madam."

Taking a sip, she thought through the various tastes as they hit her tongue and said, "Umm. Raspberry and . . . banana. A hint of, is that vanilla yogurt? Where's the kale? I'm disappointed. To me it's not a smoothie unless there's kale." This was a game they'd played a hundred times, imitating and mocking the pretentious foodies who'd taken over the strip of restaurants along Magnolia.

"Kale's so last year," Jake said, picking up on her riff. "I asked for brussels sprouts, but they were all out."

They both laughed at this.

"You better get your mom to take care of that," she said.

She tapped at the table with both hands, grinning at Jake, unable to contain the energy inside herself. She could see by the inquisitive angle of his gaze that he was trying to get a bead on why she was so excited.

"Everything okay, Elena?"

She held up a finger, like, wait a second. She felt like a hundred firecrackers were going off at the same time inside of her, each one a new thing she wanted to tell him, all of them erupting on top of each other, drowning each other out. To calm herself down, she guzzled her smoothie through the straw until she'd given herself a brain freeze. Then she threw herself dramatically, head and shoulders and one slapping open hand, onto the table.

"So," she said. And she grinned at him.

"It's good to see you, too," he said, matching her grin for grin.

Sitting up, leaning back, both hands splayed flat on the table, she just kept grinning.

"What, Elena? Tell me!" he said, carving a little doodle of expectation in the air with his head.

"It's nothing. It's stupid," she said.

Jake's eyebrows raised slightly, then returned to neutral.

"I've been talking to some guy on AnAmerica. Chatting. Like internet-wise. And . . . I don't know. It's silly. It's just flirting. Forget it."

"You've been chatting with a guy online? Don't you do that every day with your AnAmerica friends?"

"Yeah, but this is different."

"Different how?"

"I don't know. It just is. He seems smarter than most of those people. And he really liked the animation I made for you. He said it reminded him of the art he saw in Paris. He just . . . surprised me, I guess."

Jake hunched down in his chair, as much as was possible with his long legs. He had that look on his face that he got when was listening closely, taking everything in and absorbing it in that sensitive way of his. "Paris, huh?" he said.

"Yeah."

"And you've fallen in love with him because—"

"Love? Who said anything about love? I've fallen into witty banter with him. I've fallen into *Wow, you know about art and you can talk to me about my animations in a really sophisticated way and you think I'm talented and you're so much cooler than the boneheads and dweebs who usually like me* with him. I've fallen into *I'm bored and my sister's being a pain and my best friend is busy with his new family across town* with him."

Jake flinched a little, and Elena sort of regretted making that comment about him being too busy for her. But what had he said on moving day? That he'd call her all the time or something? Well, her cell hadn't exactly been ringing off the hook or buzzing with texts from him since then. She didn't want to admit it, but it kind of stung.

"Do you know anything else about him? Like what his name is, even?" he asked, his voice sharp.

"His name is Harlow."

"Harlow what?"

Elena stared at Jake, unable to answer. What was up with him today? This was exactly *not* how she'd thought this conversation would go.

"You've talked to him, how many times?"

"Like . . . two." Why did she feel so defensive? "Does it matter?" she asked.

"I don't know," said Jake. He shook his head and winced, thinking it through. "I'd be careful, Elena . . . Guys on the internet. Anybody on the internet, really. You can never know who they really are. Who knows what he might be up to. Stealing your information. Infiltrating your computer. Toying with you just to, I don't know, fulfill some dark little fantasy of his. He might not even be a guy. Or he might be eighty years old. Or seven. You see what I'm saying? Just . . . be careful."

"Okay, *Dad*. I'll keep that in mind," she said, hoping her tone would point out to him how weirdly overprotective he was being.

He looked so wounded somehow. It was bizarre. "I'd just hate to see you get hurt," he said.

"Have you ever seen me let myself get hurt? Look! I'm wearing Doc Martens!"

She yanked her foot up above the tabletop to show off her pink combat boots, hoping that doing so would lighten the mood. But Jake had withdrawn into one of his quiet places. Elena could never tell what he was thinking when he did that. She could see the emotions rippling on his surface, but she had no way of knowing what those emotions were. Though she knew there was no reason to, she felt bad, like she'd somehow done something wrong.

Jake's fans were beginning to show up. Kids from school, mostly—Becky Anderson, with her timid way of walking, like she didn't want anyone to see her and her signature waist-length braid; Arnold Chan, the computer whiz who'd gotten in so much trouble a couple of years ago when he'd been running tech for the graduation ceremony where Jules Turnbull's homemade sex tape had been inadvertently played; and a handful of others. Jake nodded and threw curt two-fingered waves at them.

Hoping to make peace, Elena asked, "How's life

in the fast lane? Has Cameron taken you out on the yacht yet?"

"No," he said glumly. "And even if he had . . . he's sort of aggressively proud of how rich he is, you know?"

Maybe this was why Jake was in such a mood today. Maybe he was having a hard time getting used to the idea of this new guy strolling into his life and in some way trying to replace his dad. Elena frowned sympathetically, but she wasn't sure Jake saw. She'd lost him to the hidden thoughts in his head.

She surveyed the room with its potted palm trees and tiki lamps and rasta flags. There was Seth Rothman. And Sally French. Hank Lewis. Cassie Crews. When Hannah Jones entered, Elena watched her fuss over where to sit. This happened every time Hannah showed up at one of Jake's gigs. Trying to look nonchalant with a finger tapping at her lip, Hannah paced from one part of the room to another, vying for a prime position near the stage, where she could sink her head into the cradle of her arms and gaze longingly at Jake while he played.

"Look," Elena said, trying again to coax him out of his mood. "Hannah's here to ogle you again."

This got him to at least look at her, but it didn't lighten his mood. "I've got a girlfriend," he snapped. "Sarah. Remember?"

"Still, it's nice to be wanted, isn't it?"

"Not by Hannah. Remember Lilah Bell?"

"Yeah." Everyone remembered Lilah Bell and the crazy obsessive way she'd stalked Jules Turnbull. It was the most exciting thing to have ever happened at Chris Columbus High. A warning story people told themselves when they felt themselves slipping toward making bad, bad decisions. "But—"

Jake cut her off before she could finish her sentence. "You want that to happen to me?"

He was just impossible today. "Jake," she said. "Why so defensive? This is me you're talking to."

She locked eyes with him and danced her head around, trying to coax a grin out of him. When it finally came, halfheartedly, she could tell Jake was just appeasing her. She sighed and rolled her head back to look at the imitation bamboo ceiling.

"When you want to talk," she said, "I'll be here."

"Will you? I hope so. You might be too busy." Before she could ask what that was supposed to mean, he tapped the table once with his fingertips and walked to the stage to tune up his guitar.

As he wandered away, she realized that this must be a reference to her online chats with Harlow. Was that it? Was Jake jealous? But why? It wasn't like some guy she'd met online could ever come between them.

Beneath his carefully cultivated casual stage per-
sona, a destructive energy surged in Jake's blood. He felt
out of control in a way that he usually never did. He
wanted to take the water bottle next to him and whip
it across the room. He wanted to pick up his stool and
shake it above his head, roaring at the audience, scar-
ing them with his rage. He wanted to smash his guitar
over Elena's head. Or his own head, because really, he
wasn't mad at her, he was mad at himself. Nathaniel was
right. He was a coward. And with this Harlow guy in the
picture now, he'd lost his chance yet again. Jake was the
kind of guy who swallowed his emotions, endured and

suffered and lost and lost again.

As he sang the first song in his set, a ballad called "I'm Here" that he'd written years ago, Jake ignored the crowd and stared moodily at his fingers. They wouldn't notice. He often looked inward as he played his music, disappearing into the feelings he conjured out of his instrument.

He played "Nothing Doing."

He played "Wake Me When You're Home."

All these old songs he knew so well he wouldn't have to think. Thinking was too much for him right now. It was like white light, blinding and obliterating him.

Every time he felt the urge to look up, he felt Elena's presence at the side of the stage and knew he'd gravitate to her, staring, his feeling of hurt and rejection bleeding out of him. He imagined her projecting this Harlow character into the romantic scenarios his songs described. It was too much for him. He could just imagine what an idiot he'd look like if he played the new song he'd written for her.

He launched into "Misunderstood," which pretty much summed up his feelings right now.

When this one came to an end, he knew he couldn't ignore the crowd much longer and he finally looked up and, leaning into the mic, said, "Thanks for coming out tonight, folks."

Forty or fifty faces gazed back at him. His fans. It was ironic—he should have been happy to see so many expectant, appreciative people here to see him, but somehow they and their devotion didn't count. All that counted was Elena, and she'd gone and found some random stranger on the internet to swoon over. Jake tried to block her out of his vision, but he couldn't. She'd dressed in her best spunky clothes—her pink Docs, those skin-tight black tights that made it so hard for Jake not to stare at her luscious legs, those layers of tank tops in differing colors and degrees of looseness that seemed always to be on the verge of falling off her body. It wasn't fair. He knew she'd gone to this effort for him. And she was so unfathomably beautiful, sitting there, watching him play.

The next song on his playlist was "Driftwood." He doodled on his fret board, procrastinating, knowing that revealing his love now, in an achy, moony emo song, would be just about the worst move he could make. She'd laugh at him. She'd think he was joking. Worse, she'd think he was endorsing her new quasi-relationship.

Jake was glad not to see Nathaniel's smirking face in the crowd. He didn't want to admit it, but Nate had been right. The good guy always lost. You had to be an asshole to win at love.

He brought his hand crashing against the strings, a loud power chord like he almost never played. Maybe if he took Nathaniel's advice, she'd see that he was worthy of her attention. She'd see he was capable of surprising her too; that he wasn't the asexual platonic BFF she saw him as.

"I'm going to mix it up a little now," he said. "This one goes out to Elena."

He threw her a defensive glance and she beamed back at him, that pure joyful smile she sometimes allowed herself brightening her face, framed adorably in her wave of black ringlets. Every time Jake saw her smile like this he was stung by its beauty, its tenderness. Nobody, not even his dad, believed in him the way Elena did. And that was the problem, wasn't it? Protecting his friendship with Elena meant he was perpetually frustrated by the distance between what they had together and what he wanted.

"Wednesday's Girl." That's what he would play. It was one of the first songs his dad had ever taught him. A mean little Bob Dylan–inspired thing his father had written about the woman who'd broken his heart before he met Jake's mom.

He strummed quickly at his guitar, generating a vigorous rumble of sound, and then he sang:

On Monday, when the world was new
She marveled at a bird that flew

Through her doorway, into her room
And spread its wings
To show her all its precious things

Oh, I warned her it was too good to be true.
I said, he's not pretty, he's just new

Glancing up, he could see from the crimson color of her face that she was hurt by this. It gave him a little thrill to think that she might experience a touch of the rejection he was feeling. He strummed on. He strummed harder. He broke a string, he strummed so hard.

On Tuesday, he was in her bed
Cooing softly, spinning thread
He bit her ear until she bled
And still she wanted to believe
In him and all his precious things.

Hearing an abrupt thump from the corner of the room where Elena was sitting, Jake looked up. She'd stood up. She was slamming shut the flap on her messenger bag. She was stalking out of the café.

"Hey . . . Elena, wait," he called after her.

But with a flip of the bird behind her back, she was already gone.

Jake felt like an idiot. The urge to chase after her and apologize was so strong that he almost fell off his stool. But he kept on strumming. He was trapped on the stage, and anyway, he had a responsibility to his fans.

10

Later that evening, Elena and Nina walked slowly around the block, looking at the Christmas decorations, the sleds on roofs and cactuses and palms wrapped in blinking lights and plastic snowmen lodged on perpetually green lawns. They paced themselves so Nina wouldn't get overheated. Elena felt like she had ants under her skin. She couldn't keep still.

"You gonna tell me what's wrong?" Nina asked her.

"Is it that obvious?"

"Of course it is. You're a Rios, girl. We're hot-blooded."

"Well, okay, fine," Elena said. She launched into a long, overheated harangue about everything that had happened tonight. The smoothie, the horrible, tense conversation in which Jake sat there and petulantly criticized her for talking to Harlow, and then that song, that unbelievably angry and just plain mean song.

"Can you believe that, Nina? Suddenly he's got all kinds of money and he moves across town and what happens? He turns into somebody I don't even know."

Nina just smiled at her like it was all a joke, but if so, Elena wanted to ask, *What's the punch line?* She didn't get what was so funny about it.

"I want my Jaybird back," she said. "The one who makes me laugh. The one who encourages me to dream big. Not the one who dogs me for talking to guys online and treats me like I'm an idiot."

Nina tipped her head, still smiling that smile, still acting like it was all just so, so funny.

"What?" Elena asked.

Nina kept on smiling.

"What's so funny? Why do you keep looking at me that way?"

They'd come out for this walk in part because Nina felt like she was up for it for once, and in part because Elena hadn't been able to sit still at home, where her father had demanded total quiet while he did the books for his Laundromat empire. It was ten thirty at night and most of the bungalows in the neighborhood were closed up, the lights completely off, or at most, a pale flicker of TV peeking out of an arched window.

"You really don't know," Nina said.

"Would I be asking if I did?"

Nina sighed and rested herself against a white fire hydrant.

"He's in love with you, mami."

"Come on. Be serious," Elena said. Hearing this at any other time, she would have laughed, but tonight she was in too much of a mood for laughter.

Nina shrugged. "Don't believe me. I couldn't care less."

"He's like my brother," Elena said. She scrunched up her nose and gagged at the thought.

"Your brother who wants to get all gooney goo-goo with you." *Gooney goo-goo* was their sisterly code for hot, sweaty sex. "What did you expect," Nina went on. "You think guys just decide they want to be friends with you? That's not how guys think." She'd worked up a sweat despite the cool night air and she wiped her brow with the sleeve of her sweatshirt. "They all want the same thing. Especially the ones who pretend not to."

"God," said Elena. Then she thought about the vision of the world her sister had just described. It was so cynical. It made her angry. "No," she said. "You know what? Maybe the dirtbags you pal around with think that way. Maybe Matty and his narco friends—"

"Matty's not no narco."

Elena couldn't tolerate the idea of her sister dragging

Jake down into the mud where she lived. Not tonight. Tonight had been bad enough already. She said it again. "Matty and his narco friends. Maybe they think like that, but Jake doesn't. Jake's got class."

"Whatever you say, Elena." Nina kept on smiling that secret smile, like she knew better and nothing Elena would say was going to change it.

"Will you stop it?"

"Stop what?" There it went again.

"Stop smiling!"

"I'm not smiling."

But Nina was. She wouldn't stop. And as long as she was smiling in that way, Elena knew, she was implying she thought Elena was naïve.

"Just . . . ," Elena said. "You know what? Screw you."

She stalked off, knowing her sister wouldn't be able to keep up.

She heard her sister call after her, "Elena, wait for me. I might need your help getting back," but she didn't care. Or she did care, but she couldn't stand being in Nina's presence any longer.

Elena picked up her pace.

The houses in their neighborhood all looked the same, Spanish-style stucco bungalows. The only way to differentiate them was by the varying colors they'd been painted. Elena knew that they were almost halfway around the block because they were coming up on the crazy glossy purple house directly catty-corner from their backyard. It would be a long walk for Nina.

Now the guilt set in. She couldn't leave her sister behind. Propping herself on a fire hydrant, Elena stopped and waited.

She longed to call Jake. To ask him if Nina's suspicions were true. But what would she say? Anyway, it was absurd. Jake wasn't in love with her. He'd seen her belch. He'd heard her fart. He'd laughed with her as she worked out why she felt so bored and unfulfilled by Ricky Thomas and Brandon Stram, the two boys she'd dated briefly during freshman and sophomore year. They'd talked about what a relief it was not to have to try and impress each other—not to have to deal with the other person trying and failing to impress you—how they could actually be themselves with each other.

No way would he betray her by falling in love with her.

11

ELECTRA AND THE EMO BOY

A bright, warm day. *The sun is out, not a cloud in the sky. The palm trees sway in the breeze—look out, there's a coconut falling, plop, onto the sand. The waves come in and the waves go out with the rhythmic murmuring of peace everlasting. Children splash in the shallow water along the shore. A sailboat floats past in the lazy, hazy distance.*

But Jaybird's not smiling. Jaybird frowns. Jaybird winces. Jaybird stares straight ahead and strums his guitar. Tall and emaciated, he hunches in a T-shirt two sizes too small and jeans that hang off his sharp hips. He clutches the guitar like it's his last hope on earth and a sad, sad song floats from the strings. When he opens his mouth to

73

sing, his Adam's apple bobs up and down, up and down.

Here comes Electra, dressed for fun in the sun. Her eyes are rimmed with black in stark Egyptian lines, like always. Her blue-black hair is as spiky as ever. But the yellow-and-red polka-dot bikini she wears today, and the bamboo skirt around her waist, and the bells jingling around her ankle, and mostly, the swaying and shimmying of her hips, say she wants to have fun, fun, fun. She dances in a circle around him. She reaches out a hand. Come join me, Jaybird.

Jaybird lets himself be coaxed into dancing, for a moment, but then he drops Electra's hand and goes back to singing his sad song.

And as he sings, a rain cloud floats slowly across the beach, a small one, a disk of gray. It's headed toward Jaybird. But along the way, it soaks Electra to the bone. She frowns under the wet hair hanging in her eyes and a squiggle of coal rises from her head.

Exit Electra. She's no longer dancing.

And Jaybird just goes on singing his sad song.

The cloud finds him like it was looking for him. It hovers above him, drenching him. He takes a duck step to the right. The cloud follows. To the left. The cloud follows. He stands in one place and lets the rain fall over him.

And he goes on singing his sad, sad song.

Here comes Electra again. She's got a cake with her

now. Iced in blue, rimmed in white. She holds it up to Jaybird.

He takes a bite, frowns, and goes back to singing his song.

Electra's written something on the cake. "Play with me, Jaybird. Life is supposed to be fun."

Jaybird doesn't bother looking at the words. He's busy. He's sad. He's singing his song.

Anyway, the rain pouring down washes them away. Electra watches as the cake grows soggy and crumbles from her hands. A single tear drips down her cheek.

Jaybird doesn't notice. He's too busy singing. He's too busy being sad. He's so in love with his sadness.

She leaves again.

The rain washes down on Jaybird. All around him, the world still frolics in the sun.

This time when she returns, she's carrying banners and flags. She races around him, waving them every which way. She pulls out a noisemaker and blows it at him. The candy-colored tube unfurls in his face.

But he just goes on playing his sad, sad, sad song.

She lights off fireworks. They explode in the sky.

Jaybird ignores them. He plays on.

When she points a firework above his head, his rain cloud soaks it and tamps it out before it can explode.

Electra crumples to the sand. She sits and she watches

Jaybird soak in the rain. She watches as the sand below him grows damp and soft. She watches as he slowly sinks in, up to his knees, to his waist. She reaches out to him, to help him pull himself up, but he doesn't take her hand. He keeps right on singing and he keeps right on sinking.

And Electra despairs. Her face, usually so white, begins to change color. It's turning blue, slowly, and puffing up. Now she's sad, too. And the longer she watches Jaybird play his sad song, the bigger she puffs. The bluer she turns. Until he's sunk so far that just his shoulders and head are above ground and she's finally blown up like a balloon.

And she pops and the tears explode out of her body and come raining down over everything.

Does Jaybird notice?

He does not. He's too busy being sad. Sinking. Disappearing in the sand under his rain cloud.

Jake had watched the animation at least a hundred times. Each time it came to an end and the Jaybird character that was supposed to be him sank under the sand, he started it again. It was one thirty in the morning now, and as he sat in his underwear at the too-small desk he'd inherited with his new room, he still couldn't bring himself to stop clicking back and watching the animation one more time.

What stung wasn't that Elena had transformed her anger at him into art like this. That was how she processed her feelings, and anyway, he knew he deserved it. He'd thrown the first punch when he'd let his emotions boil and burn at his show. When he'd taken Nathaniel's stupid advice and recklessly played that cruel song for her. What stung was that she hadn't been able to read his mind and see that he'd lashed out to hide his overwhelming love for her. Instead of bringing Elena closer, he'd pushed her away.

Jake watched the animation again. His eyes were bleary from watching so many times. He had tunnel vision from staring at the screen in the darkness. He could feel the tiredness in his cells. But still, his brain was hot and sparking, wide-awake.

The worst part was the comments. All those fans of Electra who were so eager to turn on Jaybird despite the way they'd adored him before.

"I know guys like that, Electra. They can find a way to be depressed by anything. Even videos of kittens can't cheer them up."

"Jaybird, dude. Lighten up."

Like they were talking to him. Like they didn't realize that the character in the video was a cartoon.

A new one popped up. Jake scrolled down to read it. Because what if that annoying image of a flaming motorcycle showed up, along with Harlow's name? He just had to look. It would crush his heart, he knew, but somehow he couldn't stop himself. He didn't know why.

And there it was. An aerodynamic crotch rocket shooting flames out its back end. Harlow, or whoever the guy really was, didn't even have the class to choose a cool vintage cycle like a Triumph or one of those '60s BMWs. Jake braced himself for the message he was about to read.

"Love it. What did I tell you about emo guys? You're better off without him, Electra."

You're better off without him. The words seared through Jake's mind. He couldn't get rid of them. It was like Harlow had branded them there with a hot iron. The possible repercussions of this note tapped through his head. She might believe he was right. And then what?

His thoughts veered toward worst-case scenarios. By pushing Elena away, Jake had shoved her right into the arms of this douche bag. And now Jake would never have a chance to tell her the truth about his feelings. He'd lose her completely. And it would be his own fault because if he had just suppressed his feelings like usual and screwed on a brave supportive mask, she'd never have begun to question their friendship.

Jake saw her face floating in his mind—her beautiful black eyes sparking with life, her smooth round tan cheeks, that guarded joy that flitted across her face when she was half-charmed by something he'd done. He couldn't bear the thought of never seeing that look again.

And who was this Harlow guy anyway? What did he have that Jake didn't?

Tapping at the keyboard with shaking fingers, he

Googled the name *Harlow*. He Googled the name *Harlow* with the word *Florida*. He Googled the name *Harlow* with the word *anime*. Nothing, nothing, nothing. The guy didn't exist.

He scrutinized Harlow's profile on AnAmerica. That idiotic image. A bunch of blank spaces where there should have been details about who Harlow was and then a pretty small list of things he liked: *Cowboy Bebop*, Studio Ghibli, getting lost in foreign cities, trouble, whatever that was supposed to mean. The sort of things a poseur would claim to like, for sure.

The longer Jake stared at Harlow's page, the more sure he became that this was a shell profile, made to trick Elena. *Cowboy Bebop*? Studio Ghibli? Was it any coincidence that these were the exact same things Elena liked? He must have cased her page before constructing his. No wonder he had his claws in her. It wasn't right and it wasn't fair and who knew what horrible things the guy might be up to. Poor Elena. Even if she was mad at him, Jake rationalized, he had to do something to stop her from getting hurt.

Before he'd thought it through any further than that, he had his phone to his ear and he was listening to hers ringing on the other end of the line.

"Ung. Wha . . . ," she mumbled when she answered.

"Hey. It's me. Jake."

"Jake, it's really late."

"I know. I couldn't sleep."

"Okay," she said. "Hold on."

Jake waited for her to shake the sleep from her head. This wasn't the first time he'd called her at three a.m. There'd been a time, during his dad's worst days, before he got sober, when he'd leaned on her almost every night, talking about the newest development, how they couldn't find his dad, or how they'd had to bail him out of jail, how his father seemed so helpless and sad and totally not like the dad Jake had always known.

"What's up?" she said. "You calling to apologize?"

Jake had been so swept up in the conspiracy theory he'd begun to develop around Harlow that he'd forgotten that this was the actual root of the problem between him and Elena. Confronted with his guilt, he froze up and couldn't think of what to say.

And in that fiery way of hers, Elena filled the silence between them. "'Cause what was that about? That song! I mean, I don't even know what you were trying to say to me. You think I'm some sort of flighty, stupid girl who lets whoever comes along take advantage of her? Is that how you see me?"

"No, I don't," Jake mumbled.

"Then tell me why. It's totally not like you to do something like that."

"You're right," he said dumbly.

"So?" She waited for him to explain himself.

Jake could feel the pressure on this moment, like the whole world was pressing down on his shoulders. He knew that the right thing to do was to tell her the truth: that he loved her, that he'd been overcome with an irrational and overwhelming jealousy and that he'd lashed out stupidly. For some reason, though, he couldn't do it. The possibility of being rejected by her terrified him.

All he could bring himself to say was "I'm sorry."

"Okay," she said. "Thanks."

She still sounded guarded. "Do you forgive me?" Jake asked, his insecurity gnawing at the edges of his brain.

"Yeah, Jake. I can be a dick sometimes, too. But . . ." Her voice softened and he felt the old concern and quiet care for him filter into it. ". . . what's going on with you? Why won't you tell me? It's like you suddenly don't trust me anymore."

The pressure returned. It was even heavier than before. He thought of Harlow and remembered his initial reason for calling her.

"Have you talked to Harlow?" he asked.

"A little bit. He liked my animation," she said.

His heart raced. "He's definitely not real," he said, blurting it out in one rushed breath. "Listen, I just Googled him—"

"What are you talking about?"

"You need to know, Elena. He's not real."

"Not 'real'? Like he's my imaginary friend? Like a cartoon character? Jake. Come on. Are you still on this? I'm not an idiot."

"You know what I mean. Somebody made a fake profile. Like, they're trolling you and trying to trick you. I don't know why, but—"

"Is this why you called me? Have you been up all night thinking about Harlow? Jake, why are you doing this?"

"I'm trying to protect you."

"Have I ever needed protecting before?"

"No."

"So then stop trying." Her voice was firm, final.

"But—"

"You know what? I can't deal with this tonight."

"Elena, wait—"

She was gone before he could say any more. There was just a gaping, dark, empty silence on the other end of the line now.

Jake closed his eyes and took a deep breath. *I'm such a fool*, he thought. He set the phone down on the desk and stared at it in the blue glow of his computer screen. Then he picked it up again.

The urge to call her back made him dizzy. His finger hovered over the call screen until, finally, he broke and pushed the button.

She didn't answer. The call went to voice mail after

the first ring, which Jake knew meant that she'd rejected the call.

He pushed the button again, and again she rejected it.

He felt like she was rejecting more than just his calls, like she was rejecting the entirety of their history together.

He tried one more time and when she still refused to answer, he threw his phone across the room into one of the open boxes he still hadn't unpacked. He wasn't sure which one, which was a great relief. If he'd seen where it had landed, he'd be digging around for it, and he knew that could only make things with Elena worse than they already were.

13

It always happened at the last minute. Elena's father would get a call from the manager of one of his Laundromats saying, "I think I'm sick. I just took my temperature." There'd be coughing and a wan listlessness in the manager's voice. "I can't make it in today, sorry."

And Elena would have to take over the woman's shift. It was a tedious job. She had to just sit there, making change for the old women in their thin, flower-print smocks, and sometimes fixing a jammed machine.

Today, she was near the beach on the south side, in the Slats. Mixed in with the detergent scent rising off the washers, she could smell the salt water, so near, yet so far from the cage she was stuck in by the front door of the fluorescently bright room. To pass the time, she hung out on AnAmerica, trying not to think about the frantic call she'd received from Jake the night before and wishing Harlow would reach out to her.

She couldn't help breaking into a satisfied smirk at the sight of his flaming motorcycle icon when he finally direct messaged her. She wished Jake could see the freewheeling, expansive conversations she'd been having with Harlow. It would serve him right given how totally paranoid he was being.

Propping her computer on the empty stool across from her, she clicked open the message.

"Hey, raven hair," it said. "Would you look at something for me?"

"Like what?" she wrote back.

A streaky-blond woman in flip-flops and a wraparound skirt with tropical fruit printed on it wandered up to the counter and slipped some folded bills out of her bikini top. She pushed them through the opening in the cashier's cage.

"You've inspired me. I made a video," said the next message from Harlow.

Elena quickly gave the woman five dollars' worth of quarters. The job was so easy she didn't even have to speak to the customers to fulfill their needs.

She wrote back to Harlow as soon as the woman

dragged her laundry bag away. "Hell-za yeah, I'll look at a video from you! ☺"

"Really? It probably sucks, but . . ."

"Are you being shy?"

"I've never shown my stuff to anyone before," he wrote. Then a second message came tumbling in below this one. "It's not fair, though, for me to like your stuff so much and not let you see mine, too."

Elena's heart did a little spin as she realized the risk he was taking. Her fingers could hardly keep up with her typing. "It would be an honor."

"One sec."

A moment later, a link to a private Vimeo page came in along with another message. "I'm nervous now."

"Watching," she wrote. Then she clicked through to the Vimeo page and played his animation.

It started with blackness. Then just sound, strings, and warbling synthesizers. She recognized the song. It was by Sigur Rós. Harlow let it play for ten or fifteen seconds in darkness. Then a pinpoint of white appeared in the middle of the screen, slowly growing larger. The blackness had somehow, imperceptibly, turned into a rich dark blue, flecked with other colors—greens, yellows. It looked like it had been painted with watercolors. The pinpoint of white was big enough now to see that it was an eye.

The camera pulled back to reveal a solitary man

crouching on the edge of a skyscraper. He wore a hooded cloak, and under that, a billowing white outfit wrapped in leather straps from which hung knives and assorted other Japanese weapons: throwing stars, nunchucks. Elena knew right away that this was a ronin, one of the solitary, roguish samurai whose personal code of ethics demanded that they walk alone through the world. You didn't last long in the world of anime without learning about these mythic warriors.

And then the music soared and a million robotic men rained down from the sky and the ronin leaped into action. The next two and a half minutes consisted of an intricately choreographed ballet in which the ronin swooped and spun and danced through the air, battling it out with the robots under a full moon. It was riveting. There was no dialogue, no sound at all except for the Sigur Rós song. The color palate shifted with the mood shifts in the music.

The world around Elena disappeared while she watched. It was like she'd been hypnotized.

And then, in a daze, she realized that the animation had ended.

Blinking, she let herself take in the moment. Harlow was maybe the most talented artist she'd ever encountered on AnAmerica. It was hard to believe that he didn't know this. And now having seen what he could do, his admiration of her work meant a thousand times more than it had before.

She looked around at her surroundings. The day seemed brighter in every way than it had been before she'd watched the clip—great art always had this effect on her. The winter sun streaming in the floor-to-ceiling windows of the Laundromat had gone from turning everything a pale white to pulling out the vibrant sparkle in the steel machines. She was glad that the blond woman, way back by the jumbo washers, was the only person there to witness how overwhelmed with emotion she'd suddenly become.

Elena cued the video up and watched it again, hoping to find something smart to say about it. Wells of emotion washed through her as the music soared and spun, changing and deepening with every new color washing through Harlow's animation.

She hadn't been this touched by someone else's talent since the first time she'd heard Jake play a song he'd written. But this was different. With Jake, she'd felt like she'd been able to see through to the heart of someone fragile whom she needed to look out for, like the music was telling her, in more beautiful form, things she already knew about her closest friend.

Harlow was mysterious, more worldly than her. His art dared her to grow, to expand beyond herself. She felt proud for him—and honored that he wanted her opinion on what he'd made. She was amazed that someone who could make something this good cared so much what she thought.

When she was done watching the video for the second time, she could think of only one thing to say.

"LOVE!"

"Really? You like it?" he wrote back.

"More than I can say."

"Cool."

She waited for another communication from him. When it finally came, it said, "Would it be wrong of me to ask for your phone number?"

She typed in her number. Then, to help herself feel less awkward about what was clearly a new step in their relationship, she added, "I'm a sucker for talent."

"You and me both," he said.

14

Finally, six days after moving in, Jake had managed to get all his things out of the boxes and onto the bed, floor, and chair. He'd broken down the boxes and moved them to outside his door, though not to the garage, where Cameron had told him to put them.

Feeling like he'd accomplished something monumental, he looked around the space and, for the first time, saw how big and sterile the room really was. The brushed concrete floor felt warm and slick under his bare feet. The blond wood of the designer bedroom set had a gleam to it that reinforced the feeling that this room was made for looking at, not living in. He wasn't sure he'd ever get used to it.

Now to organize the clothes, guitar paraphernalia, graphic novels, electronic devices, photos, and random other junk he'd collected over the years (why did he need those old Pokémon cards? He didn't know, but somehow he still did) and find places for them all.

He picked up a framed illustration that Elena had given him—her avatar, Electra, scowling out from a bright red bull's-eye—and gazed at it for a moment. Just the thought of her made his heart feel like it was being poked with a thousand needles.

This cleaning binge had been meant to take his mind off of her, and until now, it had succeeded. But staring at the doodle, he couldn't help gravitating toward obsessing over her again. He sat on the pile of T-shirts on his bed and traced Electra's outline with his finger, giving in to the moody self-pity he'd been avoiding.

They hadn't spoken, or even texted, since he'd woken her up in the middle of the night two days ago. He knew he'd been an ass at the gig and now he'd made things that much worse. He knew he should be the bigger person and apologize to her, but he wasn't ready yet. What he really wanted was for her to reach out to him and say, *I miss you, I'm lost here, I know how you need me, and I need you, too.* But she wasn't going to do that.

Jake thought of her kissing Harlow. He had no idea what the guy might look like, so what he saw wasn't the kiss itself but Elena's expression, that openness, that touching quiver between her eyebrows as she gazed up at Harlow, that expression that Jake imagined in his fantasies of kissing her himself—his lips trailing down her neck and grazing her shoulders, his hands gripping her waist . . .

He didn't know why the thought of Elena and Harlow together seemed like so much more of a threat than the other guys she'd dated in the past. Maybe it was because those guys had been so obviously beneath her. When she'd been seeing Robby Clay, she used to call him "the shrimp" because he was so short, but also because he had a sort of rumpled, scrunched-up way about him. Whether she meant it or not, Jake had always felt like she was secretly telling her that he had nothing to worry about from Robby, that she'd chosen the kid because he was safe. And it had been the same with Toby Stossel. But this Harlow guy—if he was really who he said he was, which Jake still refused to admit might be true—seemed like he could actually erase the future Jake had secretly planned for himself and Elena. The guy was witty—Jake had seen this from the comments he'd posted on Elena's videos. And he'd apparently traveled the world. And he—

No. This had to stop.

Leaping to his feet, Jake threw himself back into the details of room organization. He placed the illustration on one of the built-in shelves—the one closest to the ceiling, so high that even he, at six foot four, had to stand on tiptoes to reach it.

As he positioned the frame, his hand brushed against what felt like crumpled paper up there. An origami swan. This was the fifth or sixth one he'd found hidden around the room. It was odd. Nathaniel didn't seem like the kind of guy to do arts and crafts. He crushed this one and threw it into the trash bag with the others.

To fend off the nostalgia and maudlin wishes that looking at more framed photos and artwork might bring, he focused on his clothes. T-shirts in one drawer. Shorts in another. In the process he collected three more swans.

He could feel someone lurking in the doorway, watching him. An aura. A tight white heat. He knew without looking that it was Nathaniel. Jake wondered how long his stepbrother had been watching him. The guy seemed to always be there, wandering in and taking up Jake's space, watching, making quasi-helpful but mostly annoying comments about the best and worst ways to do things. Pressuring him for updates on the Elena situation.

Jake ignored him. He folded his jeans and lightweight pants and placed them in stacks in the bottom drawer.

"Looking good, brother," Nathaniel said.

Jake arched an eyebrow and glanced at him. "Thanks."

"A clean room's important," Nathaniel went on. "You

don't want to be one of those mama's boys who don't know how to pick up after themselves." Jake braced himself for the lecture on how to be suave and oily that he knew was coming. "When your chicky comes to visit—Elissa? Alana?"

"Elena."

"Right. She's going to be sizing up your room and looking for evidence. You want her to think you're interested in more than just sports and comic books."

"I'm not interested in sports," Jake said flatly, hoping his tone would convince Nathaniel to leave him in peace.

"Sure. Cool. But you've got that." Nathaniel pointed one overly manicured finger at the scale model of *Serenity*, the ship from *Firefly*, lying on its side next to the stack of framed photos on the desk.

Jake took his time responding. He picked up a stack of socks and shoved them into the top drawer of the dresser.

"She's not going to judge me for that," he said. "She gave it to me."

Instead of looking for Nathaniel's reaction, Jake kept to his task. He carried the boxers folded on the bed to the dresser and made room for them next to the socks. Two more swans. This would be the opportune time to ask Nathaniel about them, but Jake didn't want to give the guy the satisfaction of explaining their significance.

He crumpled them in his fist and shoved them into the trash bag with the others.

"What about that?" Nathaniel said. He was pointing at the photo at the top of the stack, a blow-up of Dave Matthews and Jake's dad playing acoustic guitar together in a little club in Chapel Hill, North Carolina. It was signed and everything. One of Jake's most prized possessions. "You think she's going to be impressed by Dave Matthews?"

Jake rose up slowly from his hunker over the dresser. He could feel his face going red like it did whenever he felt like he might lose his temper. "Is there something you want? Or are you just here to annoy me?" he said, conscious that if he was really going to stake his claim on his privacy, he should have found a stronger way to do it.

Nathaniel smirked at him. "Am I annoying you?" he said.

"Yes."

"Sorry, bro."

He folded his arms across his chest and hugged his palms with his armpits, a smug, closed-lipped smile frozen on his face in a way that Jake knew was a dare.

Two could play that game. Jake puffed up his chest and smiled back.

They faced off like that for a minute. Every few seconds, Nathaniel relaxed his face and screwed up his smile a little tighter. He wouldn't give.

Jake's cheeks were burning up. He hoped Nathaniel didn't call him on it.

Finally, Jake said, "So maybe you could find some-one else to annoy."

"I don't think so. This is too much fun," said Nathaniel.

"Seriously. Go."

Nathaniel mugged his shock at this, reeling his head back dramatically, that smile still arrogantly plastered on his face. "Are you kicking me out?"

"Yeah."

Bugging his eyes, Nathaniel clapped his hands together, once, pointedly.

"That's priceless. You can't kick me out, dude. This is my room."

"Not anymore," Jake said.

"Trust me. It's my room. You're living in it right now. I'll give you that. But you're only leasing it. You think you're the first person to come into *my* house and fondle *my* stuff and cuddle up under the covers of *my* bed think-ing it belonged to him now? It's almost cute how naïve you are. But you do realize you're living in fantasy land, right? You have to know this won't last. Cameron and your mother? Please. He goes through streaky blonds like her quicker than Leonardo DiCaprio. Once her wind chimey, earth goddess, kumbayah thing gets stale he'll be on to the next one. And you'll be back in that tiny ant-infested bungalow on the south side."

Throughout all of this, the smile never left Nathaniel's face. His voice never rose. He remained infuriatingly cool, barely moving from his perch against the doorway.

"So, you know," Nathaniel said, now wandering into the room and poking around Jake's stuff, "enjoy it while it lasts."

With this, he picked up the framed photo of Jake's dad and Dave Matthews and studied it for a second before raising it above his head and bringing it smashing down against the hard corner of the dresser, shattering the glass, busting the frame, ripping a deep gouge in Dave Matthews's face. Lobbing what remained of the photo onto the bed, he patted Jake on the shoulder.

"See ya," he said, and he sauntered out, leaving Jake too shocked to say or do anything.

15

Winter was Elena's favorite time to go to the beach. The tourists clung to the areas around the hotels and most of the locals in Dream Point weirdly thought it was too cold to hang out all day in their bathing suits. If she stuck to the south side of the public beach, where the promenade faded out and the driftwood and sea slime were less diligently combed away, she could find pockets where she felt almost alone. She'd been lying out for an hour already today, and except for the lifeguards changing shifts, not one person had come within a hundred yards of her.

The sun washing over her closed eyes felt warm and comforting. She let the sensation carry her off into a state of near sleep in which she was aware of the way each passing cloud affected the sensations playing over her skin.

She was aware of the squeals and shouts of distant children playing in the waves, the dense, slightly sour smell of kelp and salt water. At the same time, she felt herself floating somewhere far away where her mind retreated from the facts of her life—her sister's petulance and self-pity, her father's stern, inflexible attempts to hold their family together, and Jake, oh, Jake, what had happened to them? Everything felt far away and not quite real, and as long as she stayed here on this warm beach, she could almost feel like none of it mattered.

She could focus on the good. On Harlow and the online conversation they'd had the other day. He'd told her about the trip to Japan he'd taken last year, about how he'd made a careful plan and reached out to the biggest animators there, making sure they saw his face and learned his name.

"You can do that, too," he'd said, when she'd mentioned that she'd be too nervous to put herself out there like that. "You've got the talent. You just have to believe you deserve it," he'd told her.

She thought about the bold way he attacked his life, leaping toward what he desired as though the world was his to take and do what he wanted with. And what did he desire? Art! And did she dare think, maybe, her! For now she was playing it cool. He still hadn't called her, after all.

"There you are."

She opened her eyes and blinked in the bleached whiteness of the day. When her eyes focused, she saw Jake standing over her, dangling the yellow Cons she'd painted with cartoon monsters for him by their heels from two fingers.

"Hey," she said. She sat up and waited to see if he was going to be the old Jake she loved or this new one who picked at her and criticized and burned with judgment.

He plopped down next to her and sat cross-legged on the sand. "I stopped by your house," he said. He picked up a strand of damp seaweed and fidgeted with it, ripping off little pieces and dropping them into a pile between his legs. "Nina said you were here."

"Yup," she said, giving away nothing. "I'm here."

He picked at the seaweed. She could tell from his awkward quietness that he was anxious. He seemed afraid to look at her.

Eventually, he mumbled something. She knew what he'd said. He'd said he was sorry. But she didn't want to let him off the hook that easy. "I can't hear you, Jake," she said.

He cleared his throat. "I'm sorry," he said, more clearly now. "I . . ." Finally, he looked at her and she could see real torment in his eyes. "The way I behaved the other night. It was wrong. You . . ." She could see the words form and dissolve in his mind as he struggled to explain himself. "It was wrong," he said again. Then he gazed at her sadly, waiting for her to rescue him.

She couldn't help but smile, just briefly. This was the old Jake she knew so well. "It's okay," she said.

He winced and squinted his eyes at her. "It's not okay," he said.

"It is," she said. "But—" She gave him a soft, friendly punch on the shoulder and ducked her head playfully like a boxer. "What the hell, Jake? You know?"

Thinking deeply about the question, taking it seriously, he tore the seaweed apart some more and said, "I'm having trouble adjusting. The new house. The new people." He gazed up at the clouds and then back down at his seaweed. "And . . ." He took a deep breath and exhaled loudly. "No, you know what, I'm just sorry. That's all I wanted to say." He looked at the seaweed again and then lobbed it away, turning himself so that he was facing her. "How are you?" he said, forcing himself into a brighter place.

"I'm good. The ladies have been calling in sick at the Laundromats like they do every Christmas, so I've been filling in. Helping my dad. How's life with Cameron?"

"I'm getting used to it. Apparently he's got a son. Nathaniel. Weird no one mentioned that to me before, huh?"

She made one of her goofy faces at him to show him she understood how jarring this must have been for him. Then she said, "What's he like?"

"Like you'd expect. Spoiled rich kid."

"Invite me over. I'll set him straight," she said.

"Ha," Jake said. "I'd love to invite you over. I'm still figuring out the rules of that place. It's so . . . sterile. You know? It doesn't feel like a place where you're allowed to just hang out with your friends."

"We'll fix that, too," she said. "It's your house now. You can make your own rules."

He laughed nervously at this idea, scooping up a handful of sand. He watched it dribble out between his fingers.

"How's Harlow?" he asked, the tone of his voice just edgy enough to get under Elena's skin.

"That depends. Are you asking me as a friend? Or my protector? Which is it, Jake?"

He was doing funny things with his face, like he was fighting off a hundred contradictory impulses at once. "I'm sorry, Elena. I'm not trying to be weird or mean or anything. And I don't want to fight. But I just . . . I can't let you get hurt. I feel . . ."

Suddenly he stopped talking, like something was stuck in his throat.

"Spit it out, Jake. You've gone this far, say whatever it is you're trying to say."

"Okay, look. I'm ninety-nine-percent positive this is some sort of fake profile. I've done a lot of online searches and can't find anybody named Harlow anywhere south of Orlando."

Elena felt the sudden desire to cover up her bikini with a towel. Flopping onto her back, she reminded herself to resist the temptation to let her emotions spin into the overwrought, melodramatic place that she and her family so often indulged themselves in at moments like this. But she couldn't help it. She spun onto her side and glared at him.

"I thought you said you were sorry," she said. "What happened to wanting to be supportive?"

"I am being supportive," he said.

"By Googling him? By cyberstalking him? Do I need your permission or something to talk to a boy? It's like you move to the rich side of town and suddenly you don't want good things to happen to me."

"That's not what I meant," he said. "Elena, I'm trying—"

Now he looked betrayed, which wasn't fair at all.

"You want to know how real he is? Okay, fine. Let's talk about how real he is." She flipped the backpack she'd been using as a pillow over her head and dug angrily around in its large single pocket until she found her phone. "How's this for real?" She punched at the screen until she'd pulled up the page she'd bookmarked in the web browser. "Here. Look."

Pushing play, she handed the phone to Jake and waited for him to watch the animation Harlow had sent her. Jake leaned in on his long neck to peer at the screen. She could just hear the Sigur Rós song begin to play.

"He made that. For me. Is that real enough for you?"

Jake squinted at the screen. Elena searched his face for reactions to what he was seeing, but all she could discern was his intense concentration.

"And also, for your information, I talked to him for like three hours last night," she lied, spinning the fact that she'd given Harlow her number into a more dramatic event in hopes that this would shake Jake off the topic for good. "On the phone. Like, I heard his voice and he heard mine. He's not some weird old man. He's not a girl. He sounds just like you'd think he would. So."

He was still watching the video. Not responding.

"Can you hear me, Jake? He's really who he says he is. He's totally real."

Nothing. She wasn't sure what reaction she wanted to get from him. Something more than this.

When the clip finally ended and he handed the phone back to her, Elena realized that he was close to tears.

"Okay," he said softly.

She felt torn. The part of her that cared deeply for Jake wanted to reach out and comfort him, but the part of her that felt betrayed by his obsession with proving that Harlow was a troll needed him to promise let it go.

"Jake?" she said.

"Okay, he's real."

He tried to smile but she could tell it was a struggle for him and she knew he was retreating inside himself in that way he sometimes did.

"Thank you," she said primly. "Maybe we can get past this now."

Reaching out, she touched his hand to let him know she was ready to forget it, but as soon as her skin made contact with his, he pulled his hand away.

Elena's thoughts suddenly flashed on the conversation she'd had with her sister. Maybe Jake really was in love with her. She'd never thought of him in that way—she loved him, sure, but with a tenderness that had nothing to do with sex. She didn't get all wound up and frantic around him the way she'd watched Nina get around Matty. Their friendship was too important to let it be ruined by the crazy volatile complications that physical desire would cause.

He felt the same way. She knew he did. For one thing, he already had a girlfriend, Sarah, and he loved her enough to write song after song about her. For another thing, they'd laughed a hundred times before about how absurd it would be for them to get together. It seemed weird. It seemed icky. "It would be like incest," he'd said a few years ago, and she'd agreed.

Elena decided that he must be having trouble adjusting all the changes in his life, having Cameron around and this new brother, Nathaniel. She'd let him deal with it in his own way. When he was ready, she was sure, he'd let her back into his life, into his new house, and everything would be normal again.

Now what she needed to do was protect him. Protect them.

"You know what I've been thinking?" she said, making sure she projected a sparkling, impish smile. "It's been, like, years since we raced to the jetty. Come on." She leaped to her feet, kicking up sand, and swung her arm over her head, beckoning him to join her. "Loser buys the winner smoothies."

She ran ahead, her Docs slipping with each step, and when she glanced back fifty feet on, she saw, thankfully, that he was jogging behind her, handicapping himself to ensure that she won. Grinning, relieved, she lowered her head, churned her boots in the sand, and pushed forward as fast as she could toward the Ferris wheel in the distance.

16

When he got home, Jake raided the fridge in search of something sweet. Food sometimes distracted him from his worries, especially if it had the added benefit of giving him a sugar rush. He rifled through the freezer first, hoping for ice cream, maybe a nice untouched pint of Phish Food or a box of Popsicles from which he might be able to hoard all the red ones. But the freezer was empty except for a tray of chicken cacciatore, some bags of Chinese dumplings, an unopened block of butter, and a nearly empty carton of fancy olive-oil-and-rosemary sorbet, just the thought of which turned his stomach. He wished Cameron's personal shopper would just buy the trashy food that people actually liked to eat rather than all this healthy, locally sourced crap.

In the fridge, he found some cured meats and fancy cheese, none of which he'd ever heard of before. This would have to do. He cut a hunk off the baguette on the counter and began assembling a sandwich. The house was quieter than usual, which pleased him. Maybe no one was home, and for once, Nathaniel wouldn't be around to antagonize him. Jake looked forward to sitting out on the porch and picking at his guitar between bites of his sandwich, gazing out at the sea, letting the sadness crash over him.

He could feel Elena drifting away from him already, leaving him lost and disoriented. This afternoon at the beach, they'd managed to eventually have a good time, pretending that nothing had changed between them. But now that he was home, he couldn't help but dwell on the limits of their relationship. Harlow was real. He couldn't deny it anymore. And if he was everything Elena thought he was, he'd inevitably take her away from Jake. He felt like there was a howling wind echoing through his heart, a screaming sadness that nobody but him could hear.

As he carried his plate through the big open living area toward the porch, he realized he wasn't as alone as he'd thought. There were people upstairs hidden behind one of the closed bedroom doors. He could hear their voices but not make out what they were saying.

Freezing midstep, Jake tipped his head and listened. Two people. Both male. It must have been Cameron and Nathaniel. From their tone, he could tell that they were arguing.

One of them shouted, "Because I don't give a fuck!" Definitely Nathaniel.

A dread crept through Jake as he remembered his mom's quiet concern when he'd told her about how Nathaniel had destroyed his Dave Matthews photo. If this was about that, he could just imagine the petty and passive-aggressive ways Nathaniel would get back at him later.

Carefully stepping heel to toe, heel to toe, so that his Cons didn't squeak on the polished wood floors, Jake snuck up the stairs until he reached the landing halfway to the second floor. He could hear more clearly here.

"You're going to have to give a fuck." That was Cameron.

"Why?" Even without seeing the guy, Jake could hear the petulance dripping like syrup off Nathaniel's words.

Cameron made a noise. A chuckle maybe. Jake wasn't quite sure. "If you have to ask . . . ," he said.

This was a side of Cameron Jake had never encountered before, a controlling coarseness that brooked no dissent.

"Why do you care anyway? It's not like you ever care when *my* shit gets destroyed."

They were definitely talking about the Dave Matthews photo. Jake tried to block out all the ambient sounds in the house and focus.

"When your shit gets destroyed, it's usually you doing the destroying."

"Yeah. Whatever. If you'd let me stay at school over break like I usually do, I wouldn't *be able* to fuck up your charity case's shit. I'd be far away and you could go on slumming it with your new white-trash wife like you want to and everybody would be happy."

"That didn't happen, though, did it?"

"Clearly not."

"And why do you think that is?"

They were speaking in code about some long-hidden conflict. The darkness Jake had noticed between them at that first dinner seemed to be close to bursting out into the open. But Nathaniel said nothing, or nothing Jake could hear.

As the silence grew, Jake fought the urge to flee. He prepared himself to make an excuse about why he was standing on the stairs like this. *I was just heading up to the sunroom. It occurred to me that I hadn't checked out the art up here yet. This sandwich? Oh, I'd forgotten I had it.*

111

"Maybe," said Cameron, "just maybe, you'd do better making a friend out of Jake. You might just learn something."

"Ha."

"That's not a suggestion, Nate. It's a demand. Get your shit together. Jake's a good kid. Polite. I've been told he's talented. He works hard and doesn't assume anybody's going to—"

"He's a hick, Cameron. He's clueless. If you weren't fucking his mother, you'd realize he's the kind of guy who, when they come stay at your hotels, you have reception hide them away in one of the back rooms so that they don't embarrass the other guests."

Was that a slap? Jake didn't want to know.

"He's a hell of a lot less embarrassing than you."

Jake didn't want to hear any more. He shouldn't have been listening to begin with. But he couldn't stop. He wasn't sure how he felt about the way that Cameron was praising him. It was flattering, but also, this was *his son* he was talking to. If he treated his own flesh and blood this way, wasn't it possible that he'd one day turn on Jake and his mom, too? Maybe, maybe not. Jake didn't know nearly enough about the fraught history between his stepfather (and how weird it felt to call Cameron this) and Nathaniel to fully comprehend why they spoke to each other this way. The one thing he did know was that the two of them were creeping him out. He didn't want to be held up as an example of anything. Not if it meant being sucked into their toxic relationship.

"One call to my lawyer, Nate," Cameron said. "One call. And you'd realize how much less embarrassing Jake is than you."

"You wouldn't dare."

"I would and I will, if you don't wise up and stop acting like an ungrateful little bastard."

What were they talking about? Jake wasn't sure.

"You really want to get into this?" Nathaniel was shouting again. "You really want to do this? That's my money. You owe me that money. That's blood money."

Were they talking about Nathaniel's trust fund? Jake definitely shouldn't have been listening to this. It was intrusive. It was just wrong. He wished he hadn't heard as much as he had, and he hoped that it didn't mess with his head.

Tiptoeing back down the stairs, he decided not to carry out his porch-sitting, guitar-playing plan. Better for them not to know he was home. He locked himself in his room. The fact that it had once been Nathaniel's seemed more significant now. It made him uncomfortable, like he'd done something wrong without even knowing it.

He wasn't hungry for the sandwich. He didn't even know, anymore, why he'd made it. Leaving it on the desk, he lay down on the bed and tried to clear his head.

He longed to talk to Elena, to tell her about the craziness he'd just witnessed. What if she were here right now? He'd feel better. He could just see her on the edge of the bed with her chin in her knees, eyes wide in disbelief. He could hear her saying, Wow. *These are definitely rich people's problems.*

She'd be wearing that bright blue bikini she'd had on today, totally unself-conscious about how it clashed with her Doc Martens or how exposed her body was. And Jake wouldn't be able to stop himself from noticing the smoothness of her thighs, the way her strawberry mark peeked out of the lip of her bikini bottoms like it was teasing him, urging him to imagine everything else hidden there.

She'd been so beautiful today. She'd glowed. Maybe it was because she was falling in love. But why couldn't she be falling in love with him?

He imagined her leaning in and kissing his neck. He'd be unable to resist peeking down her top and she'd notice but she wouldn't make a scornful face. She'd ask him, "Do you want to see what's under there?"

And he'd nod, so full of aching desire that he wouldn't even be able to talk. She'd stare into his eyes and as she held his gaze, she'd reach behind her to untie her top.

It would be like there was a chain of energy connecting them to each other.

They'd fall into each other. They'd fall together. And they'd never hit the ground.

17

Nina and Matty had apparently made up. Elena hadn't been sure what they'd been fighting about this time, but clearly, whatever it was, they'd forgotten, because here Matty was, acting like a big man, barking at the basketball game on the television, running his hand like a comb over his faux hawk. Waving his arms and yelling for Nina to shut up every time her chatter threatened to interrupt his focus on a possibly killer play. Nina yelled right back. Yelling was their default mode. That and blasting speed metal so they had to shout every single thing they said even louder, like they thought they were in a dark, trashy bar when actually they were camped out in the living room.

Just another Monday night in Chez Rios, thought Elena as she slinked through to the kitchen to get a glass of water.

When she returned to the living room, Matty had a shot of vodka in his hand. He held it to his lips, and extended his other arm straight out like he was preparing to brace himself for a fall. Then in one swift motion he tipped his head back, swallowed the shot, and squished up his tight, angry rodent face.

Nina drank from a tall tumbler of orange juice that Elena knew from the quickly dwindling bottle of Grey Goose was spiked with vodka.

"Nina—" Elena said. She had to yell to be heard over the music.

But before she could articulate her warning, her sister barked back at her, "What? It's just juice." She stared at Elena, daring her to call her bluff, and then went on, "Anyway, we're celebrating."

"Oh?" said Elena. "What are you celebrating?"

"That it's Monday," Matty said.

"And Matty just got paid," added Nina.

Elena didn't even want to know how that had happened. She was pretty sure that they were partying— where Matty went, cocaine always followed, especially after he'd somehow landed a wad of cash, and she'd seen the telltale dust on the hub of his thumb.

"Can you at least turn the music down?" she said.

Matty shot her a shit-eating grin. "That would defeat the purpose," he said.

Back in her room, she gazed at the *Cowboy Bebop* poster. It swayed to the shaking of the wall behind it. That's how loud Matty had turned the thrash.

But what was she going to do? Get into it with Nina about how she was pregnant and should think of the child and didn't that mean anything to her? She was sick of pointing out obvious stuff, like that when things were good with Matty they started going very bad in every other way.

She just didn't have the energy tonight, and anyway, it's not like Nina would listen to her. Elena kept telling herself that being here was somehow keeping her family from falling apart, but lately, she was beginning to realize that she might be lying to herself. Did staying at home change anything or anyone? Was she just trying to live up to some expectation that her mother had? Was it all a waste of time?

There was only one thing to do. Flee. Leave the chaos behind her for her father to find when he got home at three in the morning from the Laundromat.

So that's what Elena did. She threw on her black hoodie and slung her backpack over her shoulder and slipped out the door.

Outside, the air was brisk. A little chilly. She huddled in her sweatshirt and gazed down Greenvale Street at the identical bungalows, differentiated only by the scale of Christmas decoration in their front yards. She wasn't really thinking about where she would go; instead she just let her legs take her somewhere, anywhere.

Old habits died hard. Not two minutes later, she found herself knocking on the door of the empty house where Jake used to live, waiting for him to open up and bug his eyes and say, "Nina again?" But he didn't. He wasn't there. The windows were all dark. The porch light was not only off, but it didn't even have a bulb in it anymore. And she'd have to find new ways to cope with her life.

At least she could call him now that they'd come to a tentative truce this afternoon. Jake on the phone was better than no Jake at all. He'd still be able to laugh at the absurdity of her life with her.

Digging through her backpack, she pulled out her cell. And just as she was about to dial Jake's number, it rang and it wasn't Jake. She didn't know who it was, actually.

For a second she thought maybe she shouldn't answer. But she couldn't resist. It might be Harlow.

"Hello?" she said. "Who's this?"

"Who do you think?" said a voice. It was male. She noticed that it had a tone to it, a confidence, a power.

"Harlow?"

"Hope you're not too disappointed."

Elena grinned despite her bad mood. Now that she was actually talking to him, she didn't quite know what to say.

"Am I calling at a bad time or something?" he asked.

"No, not at all. I'm just . . ." She caught herself before she foolishly launched into a harangue about Nina and Matty. She was a little intimidated by him—by actually hearing his voice. It was one thing to flirt with someone online. Talking to them for real was a whole other ball game. She didn't want him to hear her upset like this, not if it might lead him to like her less. "Hanging out," she finally said. "What's up with you?"

"Oh, you know. Just sitting here twiddling my thumbs and thinking about my favorite anime girl. You gonna tell me what's wrong?" he asked.

"Nothing's wrong. What do you mean?"

"You sound . . . edgy. Like something's going on."

Was it that obvious? She took off, speed-walking across Jake's old lawn and down the block hoping that the movement would burn off the frustration that even talking to Harlow hadn't displaced.

"Nothing's going on. Well, something's going on, but it doesn't matter. I'm fine," she said.

"You're fine. Okay. I'll believe that, like, never."

"It's stupid. I mean, it's not stupid. It's horrible and depressing and it's my life but—or, you know what, it *is* stupid. I don't want to bother you with it."

What was she doing? Babbling, that's what. She chastised herself. *Get it together, Elena.*

"That's too bad," he said, graciously overlooking the gibberish dripping out of her mouth. "I love being bothered. Other people's problems are so much more interesting than my own."

Elena hedged. She was walking quickly, not anywhere specific, just walking. As though walking fast enough would allow her to outrun her life.

"Or don't," said Harlow. "Be that kind of person."

Before she knew what she was doing, she'd said, "My sister's pregnant."

"Is she twelve?" Harlow asked.

Elena laughed despite herself. "No. She—"

"Then what's the problem?"

"I thought you wanted to listen to this."

"Sorry. Bad joke. I'll listen."

He waited, silently, as she tried to formulate how to say what she meant. It was hard to decide where to begin. While she was thinking, she tripped over a lip of sidewalk. She caught herself before she fell, and, looking around, she realized that she was near the boundary of her neighborhood. The bungalows were beginning to give way to more modern ranch-style houses. She headed uphill along Sunrise toward Seminole Park.

"She's twenty," Elena finally said. "Nina. That's her name. And I don't know. She's, like . . . really overweight.

Like, obese. I'm not trying to be judgey. It's just true. And so, fine. Whatever. She's always been big. She can't really help that. But so, she's got all these complications with the pregnancy and . . ." What was she doing? She wasn't being articulate in any way. Harlow must have been thinking she was a half-wit. "This isn't making sense," she said. "Let me start over."

"It's making sense. Just—what's that they say?—use your words," he said.

"She's got this boyfriend. Matty," she went on, anger building inside her. "He's a total shitbag. I mean, at least he's around. He didn't jump and run as soon as he found out she was pregnant, but . . . he's a fucking cokehead, and she's, like . . . I worry about her. And tonight, they were . . . Matty. He reels her in and gets her to do things that . . ."

She was crying. She felt like a total fool.

". . . and I think about that baby and . . ."

She should just shut up. Just stop now before she lost all dignity.

"So you're worried about her," said Harlow.

"Yeah," said Elena. Then she blurted out, "But she's so fucking clueless. And, like, self-destructive some-times."

"But still. You love her."

"Of course I do. She's my sister."

"That's what makes life so hard," Harlow said.

"Sometimes you don't even like the people you love, but whether you like them or not doesn't really matter. You're connected to them. You can't help but want to do absolutely anything to protect them. To make their lives better. I think about the people I've loved in my life, and I don't know, I wish I'd been nicer to them. You don't realize it right now, maybe, but you're lucky to have Nina. Even if she makes you cringe most of the time."

Listening to Harlow talk about Nina, Elena felt as though he understood exactly what she was feeling. Like if she just clung to his voice, he'd carry her through to some new, more hopeful place.

She didn't want him to ever stop talking. "Maybe I should feel lucky, but I don't," she said.

She'd reached the edge of the park. It rose up in front of her, a small man-made hill, lush with grass and trees like night sentries in the darkness.

"Harlow? Are you still there?"

"Yeah. I'm just thinking about this kid I used to know. Or, okay. He was more than a kid I used to know. He was my best friend. Corey. His name was Corey. He was a little . . . off, if you know what I mean. Like, scared of the world. He had a stutter. And he was always having panic attacks. People were horrible to him. I sort of protected him. A little bit. Not as much as I should have. It was like with you and Nina. No matter how much I secretly cared about him, when we were in public, in front of the other kids in our class, I was embarrassed by him."

Something in Harlow's voice told Elena that this story wasn't something he'd revealed to very many people. She was flattered, honored, that he'd decided to tell her. As she listened, she wandered into the park and up the steps, past the rubberized children's area where she and Jake used to play when they were kids. She was headed toward the top of the hill, thinking it might be nice to sit on the bench under the granite obelisk there. The silence and peacefulness that always surrounded that particular spot would help her focus and really hear what Harlow was saying.

"We must have been, maybe, nine. Still little kids, and . . . one day we were playing, I don't know, some stupid game. Superheroes. I was Batman and he was Spider-Man. We'd snuck up to the top of the apartment complex where he lived with his mom. And he kept saying we shouldn't be there. Getting really upset about how we were breaking the rules. I teased him. I told him he was just scared and that if we were really superheroes, we had to hang out on top of buildings, otherwise we wouldn't be able to see where the villains were hiding below us.

"I could tell he was conflicted. He wanted to impress me, wanted me to see him as something more than a charity case. But also, he was terrified. And I pushed him. I told him that we had to get right up to the edge of the building and perch there. We were eight stories up. He was afraid of heights. But he did it. He squatted on top of the safety wall at the edge of the building—it was, like, a foot wide; it was crazy what we were doing—and he looked around for the bad guys, pretending he wasn't scared, hoping I wouldn't see how his whole body was shaking with fear. And then he looked down. Like straight down. And it was like he was hypnotized and . . ."

Harlow's voice cracked and he stopped talking. Was he crying? Elena wasn't sure.

"I saw what was going to happen and I tried to . . . but I couldn't . . . I . . . I couldn't . . ."

He was definitely crying. Elena didn't know what to say.

"Sorry," he said. He let out a little sob.

She stopped climbing and stood still at the top of the hill, looking out at the grid of lights mapping the layout of the town below her, wondering where in that tangle of people he might be.

"Don't be sorry," she said. "It's okay."

She could hear his breath heaving and lurching.

"I wish you were here with me right now," she said. "So I could comfort you. And give you a hug."

The sounds he was making stopped so abruptly that Elena thought the line had been disconnected.

"Did I lose you?" she said.

Nothing. She could see the headlights of cars meandering through the streets. The Christmas lights strung through the palms along Flamingo Drive. The darkness of the water far off at the edge where the city met the beach. There was something so lonely about Christmastime in the tropics.

"Harlow?"

"I'm still here," he said. His voice was flat and solid. It was like he hadn't been crying after all.

"Are you okay?" she asked.

"Yeah."

"Are you sure? You were so upset."

"I shouldn't have done that. I shouldn't have unloaded all that on you."

"It's okay."

"It's not okay." His voice rose slightly. She sensed anger lurking inside it. "I vowed not to let myself feel things like that anymore. Feelings don't do any good. They just get you in trouble."

Her heart ached for him. Was his life so unsafe that he could never, under any circumstances, take off his armor? "Don't say that," she said. "You can feel things. With me you can."

"I've got to go," he said quickly.

"No. Wait." She'd pushed him too hard. She squeezed her eyes shut, cursing herself. Then, impulsively, she said, "I want to see you. In person. Can I see you?"

More silence. But she knew he was still there.

Finally, he said, "Christmas Eve. I'll pick you up.

We'll fly away somewhere."

Her breath caught in her throat, a tiny thrill of anticipation. Christmas Eve. That was the day after tomorrow.

"How will you recognize me? Should I text you a
photo?" she asked.

"No. I want to be surprised. You'll recognize me. I'll
be the one on the motorcycle."

"Okay. See you soon."

When he didn't say anything in response, she realized he was gone, really gone, this time.

Two days, though. She could wait that long.

Looking out over the town again, she found her
neighborhood. All those Spanish terra-cotta roofs. She
counted the streets, then the houses in the streets, making her way toward the one she lived in. Nina and Matty
would still be inside. She wondered if their partying had
turned to fighting yet. She wondered how brutal the situation would get when her dad came home and found
them drunk and belligerent. She wondered if she should
kill some more time, maybe stay out all night and not go
home at all.

From way up here in Seminole Park, with the tanta-
lizing date with Harlow dangling two days in front of her,
everything in her life felt remote and far away. She could
feel herself rising up and floating away from her problems.
Almost like they didn't matter, but of course they did.

18

Jake usually spent Christmas in the Keys with his father, but this year, because of the move and their concerns about him getting used to the new situation with Cameron, his parents had decided he should stay in Dream Point. As a compromise, on December 23— Christmas Eve Eve, is how he was thinking of it—his father drove up to spend the day with him. He would have stayed longer, but as Jake knew, he had a standing Christmas Eve gig at Rum Runners, a massive beach bar where the holiday tourists would be lined up around the block to hear him sing his old tunes. Not something he could miss, as much as he might want to.

They had lunch at Enoteca Medici, on Magnolia,

which had been dressed so completely in Christmas decorations that the place looked like giant ball of tinsel. Jake ordered a fancy leg-of-lamb sandwich. His father ordered a salad consisting of farro and dried fruits.

"A salad, Dad?" Jake said. "I thought your rule was if it wasn't fried you didn't eat it."

"Baby steps," his dad said in response. "I've gone vegan. Maybe I'm finally a grown-up."

Knowing how bad his dad felt about not being able to spend the actual holiday with him, and suspecting that his emotions surrounding Jake's mom's new marriage were more complicated and pained than he let on, Jake had been putting on a happy face throughout the meal.

"You've always been a grown-up to me," he said. "Anyway, it's a big step. I guess it goes with the new look, huh?" The old man had shaved his head and he wore a slate-gray collarless shirt that made him look almost like a Buddhist monk. "If I saw you on the street, I'd think, *There goes a guy who's found enlightenment.*"

"I don't know about that," his dad said with a wry smile. "It keeps me clean, though. The sutras are great poetry. I'm working on putting them to music. Like a song cycle."

They talked about the challenges of translating spiritual poetry into the language of rock and roll. Jake liked the way his father treated him as an equal when they talked about music. He knew it was just his dad's way of showing support, but it gave him confidence nonetheless. He was relieved, too, that they could talk about this instead of his various anxieties and conflicts. He didn't want to bother his dad with stories about Nathaniel's breaking of the Dave Matthews photo or any of the other ways the guy was trying to make his life in his new home uncomfortable.

Eventually, inevitably, his father asked what Elena was up to.

Jake dodged the question. "She's been busy with her animations," he said, glancing away. He didn't mention Harlow at all. Even with his dad, who was pretty much his best friend outside of Elena, he didn't want to look like a paranoid lunatic.

Still, he could tell that his dad sensed that something was wrong and he was glad when the old man didn't push the topic.

All in all, it was a nice, quiet yet slightly melancholy visit. After they'd eaten their desserts and his dad had downed his usual four cups of coffee, they wandered out of the dark restaurant onto the boulevard and blinked in the sunlight like they'd just come out of a movie.

"Wanna take a walk?" Jake's dad asked.

"Sure."

They meandered down Magnolia, past the upscale boutiques and specialty shops. Just two extremely tall, thin guys, taking in the baubles and wreaths the town had mounted on the lampposts, not really talking, just marking time together.

Jake felt himself relaxing like he did when he was around his dad. He felt like he didn't have to be anything but himself. It was nice, just hanging like this. It almost felt like they were having a conversation through the silence, like his dad was teaching him something about wisdom and vision.

When they hit the dead end where Magnolia opened out onto the promenade, they crossed the street and turned down the winding path along the beach. They didn't have to discuss it. They just knew it was the thing that would happen next.

"So, hey," Jake's dad said. "You going to tell me why you're so blue?"

Jake winced. "Is it that obvious?"

"I've had enough sadness in my life. I know it when I see it."

Some Rollerbladers wove past them.

"You wanna guess?" Jake said.

His father stopped walking and pursed his lips. He squinted at Jake with his icy-blue eyes like he was trying to see into his soul. "No," he said.

They walked on, slowly. Silently.

When they'd passed Harpoon Haven, which was closed for the season, Jake's dad ventured a guess. "I'd say you're in love."

Jake sighed. "I've been in love forever," he said. "It's just . . . lately, it's become excruciating."

"Have you told her yet?"

"How do you do that?" Jake said. "I don't know how to do that!"

"'Cause, what if she says she's not in love with you and instead of gaining a girlfriend, you lose the best friend you ever had?" his dad said.

It was just like him to see the whole situation without Jake having even mentioned Elena's name.

"Did you know that Cameron has a son?"

His dad raised an eyebrow. He tipped his head like he did when he was listening intently.

"Yeah, neither did I, but apparently, he does. His name's Nathaniel. He's a total prick. But he's been giving me love life advice."

"Is it helpful?"

"I don't know. He wants me to 'bro' up. He says girls are only interested in guys who treat them like shit. And that I should just make a move and force her to react."

"That's not the kind of thing the Elena I know would respond to," said Jake's dad. He rubbed his scratchy chin and half smirked. "Or, she'd respond with a boot to the ass."

"That's what I think."

"But he's right about one thing." Jake's dad stopped again. He hopped up onto the iron railing that ran along the promenade and sat there. "You should tell her. After all these years, she deserves to know."

Jake felt like he'd been called out. "Yeah," he mumbled. "I realize that."

"There are better ways to do it than playing grab bag, though. You've got talents. And you've got heart." For a second, Jake's dad's gaze floated away, like he was remembering some poignant moment from his past. "Do you have any idea how romantic a true voice and an acoustic guitar can be? You just have to trust yourself. Believe you're lovable. Your sensitivity and kindness will show through."

He chucked Jake on the chin. "Braw," he said with a wink.

Jake chuckled. "The guy really is a total dick."

"I'm sure."

His dad stared off into the distance, thinking things over. Jake knew he must be comparing what Jake had told him to his perceptions of Cameron. He'd never fully gotten over Jake's mom. And when his emotions became too strong he had a way of retreating into himself, a trait Jake had, for better or worse, inherited.

"What time is it?" he asked Jake now. "I should probably hit a meeting before it gets too late."

"Sure," Jake said. "You go. I'm going to hang out on the beach for a while. Think things through."

Hopping down from his perch, Jake's dad gave him a

little side hug. "Don't think so hard that you think your-self out of it," he said. Then he wandered ten feet or so up the promenade. "Hey," he called back to Jake, doing a little bow. "Merry Christmas."

He slid a small package wrapped in brown construc-tion paper out of his pocket and lobbed it to Jake.

As Jake caught it, his dad called out, "You thought I forgot, didn't you?"

"Never," Jake replied. Then he added, "Merry Christ-mas, Dad."

He watched his father jog away, his shirt billowing out behind him. As soon as the old man had rounded the corner past the juice bar and headed up the side street, Jake slid his finger under the taped flaps on the pack-age and carefully unwrapped it. Then, opening the box inside, he found a guitar pick with a hole drilled in one end. His father had strung it onto a cheap silver chain.

Jake turned the pick over in his fingers, studying it. It took him a minute to figure out what this present was supposed to mean. Then he saw the inscription that his dad had crudely carved into the plastic: Santana, March 12, 1998, Miami Beach Amphitheater. His father had told him about that show and how he'd been invited backstage to meet the legendary man. He must have been holding on to this pick all these years, waiting for the right time to give it to Jake. Now that he knew what it was, Jake felt a great power dwelling in the pick, like it connected him to both his father's history and the history of the music he loved.

He slipped the chain over his neck and, feeling the pick against his chest, he felt strong and confident. Worthy of Elena. Like if she saw him like this, her sense of him might be totally transformed.

He knew that if he didn't act now, he'd do exactly what his father had predicted and find some way to talk himself out of telling Elena the truth. He whipped out his phone and sent Elena a text: "CHRISTMAS DAY GIFT EXCHANGE. USUAL SPOT?"

19

Glued to the arched window in the living room, Elena peered around the side of the fake tree, watching the cars trickle along Greenvale Street, one every five or ten minutes. An Escalade, its chrome gleaming in the sunlight. A rusty old Volvo that rattled like it would collapse at any minute. Her heart beat in her ears as she waited for his motorcycle, each passing moment leaving her a touch more convinced that he wasn't coming than she was before.

Matty, who had taken up residence in the house after Elena's dad, in his exhaustion from eighteen hours straight of work, had closed his eyes and muttered silently to himself rather than kicking him out the other night, was perched on the couch watching her fret while he ate his afternoon snack of Pop-Tarts and Bud Light. He hadn't worn a shirt in two days and Elena had gotten to know the vaguely tribal tattoos snaking down his pecs better than she ever wanted to.

He wouldn't shut up. "Looks like lover boy's not coming, yo. Sucks to be you, Elena. You sure he's not just a cartoon? I bet he's just a cartoon. Maybe he got lost trying to figure out how to get out of Jellystone." On and on like this. And since Nina was hidden away in the darkened bedroom, sleeping off her hangover, Elena had no one to appeal to for help in shutting him up.

Elena didn't say a word. She knew from experience that if she took the bait it would only get worse. Trying to block his voice out of her head, she leaned her temple against the glass of the window and watched. Waited. Hoped beyond hope that Matty was wrong.

A minivan rolled past.

A Smart Car.

A motorcycle, one of those aerodynamic ones that looked like they'd flown in from the future. This one was white and red and the guy tucked onto it was decked out in white leather with red and blue highlights. He slowed down and idled in front of the house to adjust a strap on his ankle. Then he pulled off his glove and began fiddling with his phone.

The guy was disarmingly good-looking, wavy blond

hair moussed back on his head, a face like a model, both refined and masculine. It couldn't be Harlow, could it? He didn't fit the type. Elena couldn't imagine a guy who looked like this being attracted to the nerdy culture of anime. She couldn't imagine a guy this handsome existing at all.

She was so nervous she could hardly breathe. When her phone buzzed in the pocket of her jeans, it startled her so much that she let out a little yelp.

Matty laughed at her. "Lover boy's canceling now, hey?" he said from his seat on the couch. He obviously hadn't seen the cycle pull up out front.

She checked her phone. The message said, "WANNA TAKE A RIDE?"

Hell yeah, she did.

Throwing Matty two birds over her shoulders, she flew out the door trying to play it cool.

Harlow didn't wave when he saw her walking toward him. He barely even smiled. He just jutted his jaw and acknowledged her with a small nod.

"Hop on," he said, revving the engine.

She'd never been on a motorcycle before. The seat was wider than she'd expected and she felt foolish trying to sling her leg over the whole thing.

"Now hold on tight," he said.

She wasn't sure where to put her hands—behind her on the metal rail at the back of the seat? Around

Harlow's waist? That seemed abruptly intimate. Did she dare? She placed them on his shoulders, grabbing on to the leather.

"Yeah," he said. "We'll be going too fast for that."

When he uncurled her fingers from the leather, he did so with a delicacy that sent a charge through Elena's chest. He had the gloves on again, so she couldn't tell how soft his fingers might be, but they were long and thin and nothing like the pudgy peasant hands of the guys in her family. He guided her hands down and around his waist, laying them flat on his tight stomach.

"You ready?" he said.

She inched up closer behind him until she could feel his butt against her inner thighs and her chin was resting against his shoulder. He smelled like vanilla. She gulped the scent down.

"As ready as I'll ever be," she said.

And they were off. Zero to sixty in what felt like half a second. When they took the corner at the end of the block the cycle leaned so low she felt like she would fall off. She squeezed tighter. She held on with all her might. They raced forward. Zigging and zagging through the residential streets. He seemed to know where he was going, though she didn't. She felt out of control, flapping behind him, his body the only thing tethering her to the earth—it was like an iron rod between her arms, rigid and firm and totally in control. With every twist and turn of the bike, she could feel his muscles moving under the leather. They tensed and released and slid ever so slightly in this or that direction as he adjusted his balance and responded to the road.

"Where are we going?" she asked.

He didn't respond. He couldn't hear her.

She leaned in closer and shouted right into his ear, "Where are we going?"

"Anywhere," he said. "Everywhere."

They sped through the Slats. Headed downtown.

When they hit Shore Drive, he shouted, "Brace yourself!" into the wind and before she knew it her stomach was doing somersaults and they were up on one wheel.

This was crazy. They weren't even wearing helmets. But she wasn't going to complain. She couldn't have done so if she wanted to. Her words would have flown behind them, lost on the wind.

Not losing speed, he popped the curb and they were suddenly on the promenade, tearing up the grass, dodging palm trees and park benches. They followed the pathway for a while and then Harlow turned onto a pedestrian ramp that led down to the beach.

Elena shouted into his ear again. "This is totally illegal," she said.

"Do you care?" he said.

Did she? She wasn't sure. She decided that no, she

didn't care. Not one bit.

Kicking up sand, they raced along the shore, ignoring the sunbathers and water waders staring, pointing, yelling for them to get the hell off the beach. Slowing down just slightly, Harlow twisted his head back so that he could look at her. He had a cockeyed grin on his face, both alluring and brash. She could see the flecks of yellow in his brown eyes.

He slowed further and kicked his legs out from the machine so he could balance his toes on the sand. Elena wasn't sure if she was supposed to hop off or not. She didn't want to let go of Harlow.

"What now?" she asked.

He raised an eyebrow. "You tell me," he said. "Should we find someplace to sit and get to know each other?"

She felt a trill in the base of her throat like her heart was trying to jump out. "Yeah," she said, playing it cool. "Name's Elena. And you are . . ."

"Harlow."

She hopped off the cycle. Her whole body was numb and tingly from the shaking of the motorcycle between her legs. Holding out a hand, she said, "Nice to meet you, Harlow."

"Finally," he added with a wink, finishing her sentence. He pulled off his glove and shook hands with her. "You look different than I imagined," he said.

She held her arms out and did a little spin, feeling

the intensity of his eyes on her as he sized her up. "Are you disappointed?"

"I wouldn't say that."

He continued staring at her, letting his eyes roll up and down her body. She'd never in her life felt so sexualized—so wanted. His gaze was so intense that she had to look away. She wondered where they'd go. She wondered how long it would take him to kiss her.

Just as he was about to dismount, he reached into a pocket and pulled out his phone. He scrolled through his messages, his face pinched with tension. "Fuck me," he said.

"What?" she said. When he didn't answer, she asked again, "What is it?"

"I gotta go."

It was like Elena had been floating on a giant balloon and someone had come along and abruptly popped it.

"Why? What happened? Is everything okay?" she asked, hoping her disappointment didn't show through too obviously.

"I can't talk about it. Just . . ." He shook his head a couple times like he was trying to dislodge some worry. "There's trouble. But I'll be fine."

When he looked at her, something heartbreaking sparked in his eye. And she knew she couldn't ask more from him than she already had. She wished she could reach out and hold him. Make whatever it was that was happening go away.

"Come here a sec," he said. "There's something I've been wanting to do."

She took two steps toward the bike and he put his hands on her waist, pulling her urgently toward himself. He had her pressed up tight to him and before she even comprehended what was happening, he was kissing her, deeply, intensely.

She was shocked for a second. Then a thrill surged through her entire body and she relaxed and gave in to the sensation of his lips against hers. Just as she began to kiss him back, she felt a quick pain in her bottom lip. He'd nipped her with his teeth.

He did it again.

And then he let her go, dropping her, and she realized that she'd been off her feet this whole time. She'd been so startled by what was going on that she hadn't even noticed until now.

"Nice to meet you, Elena," he whispered.

He caressed her cheek with the flat palm of his hand.

Pulling his glove back on, he bent over the motorcycle and revved the engine.

He didn't look in her direction again. Instead, he spun a circle in the sand and raced off the way they had come.

Elena just stood there, watching him go, thinking, *Oh my God. What was that? What just happened?*

Her lip tingled from where he'd bitten her. She felt supercharged by the mix of adrenaline, vibrations from the bike, and the emotional echo, still wavering inside her, from the kiss that had ended much too soon.

Patting Cameron's forearm, Jake's mother reminded him it was Christmas Eve. "We've got so many reasons to be happy," she said, glancing meaningfully at Jake. "Don't let Nathaniel ruin the holiday. You'll just be giving him what he wants."

"I won't," Cameron told her, but the edge in his voice implied that he already had. "But, really? How do you get booted from the Roderick School? They're used to dealing with overweaned fuckups. That's what we pay them for."

Here we go again, thought Jake, staring out the window at the silvery-pink water, trying not to get involved.

They were seated in plush white leather chairs at the

exclusive back corner table at the Spanish Armada, the fanciest restaurant in Dream Point, right on the water on a peninsula that curved into the ocean on the north side of town in a converted antebellum-style building that, if the legends were true, had once been used as a kind of money-laundering bank by pirates. The dark, moody leather and wood interior of the space had been spruced up for the holidays with discreetly placed wreaths and tableaus of holly and candles.

It was almost six. They were on their fifth and sixth plates of prime rib, lobster, sushi, and roast goose from the luxurious holiday all-you-can-eat buffet and Nathaniel had yet to make his appearance.

Cameron poured himself another glass of pinot noir, his fifth—filled right up to the top. "It's his life. He can waste it if he wants," he said. Jake had never seen him drink like this. "At least now we know why he's so afraid to show his face."

"He passed gym," Jake's mom said, and Cameron gave one abrupt, arch laugh. She was in full-on management mode, her voice peppy and soothing, like a captain refusing to admit that the ship was going down. Jake couldn't help thinking about all those times she'd acted this same way with his dad. The difference was that Cameron was brooding over things outside himself while Jake's dad had been more likely to be getting lost in his own sense of failure. His mom had barely touched her champagne except to fish the raspberry out of it with her spoon.

"Of course he passed gym. How does someone not pass gym?" Cameron took a long gulp of his wine. "What I want to know is how he failed economics. If you're gonna run a black-market Adderall business out of your dorm room, you should at least know how to play the margins." He shook his head ruefully and ran his hand through his mane of hair. Then, holding a shrimp up by its tail and studying it like it contained some runic message, he said, "I should never have purchased that drugstore chain."

Jake couldn't help noticing that, even in his blackest mood (and Jake had never seen him angrier than he was today), Cameron's mind still fired on multiple cylinders at once. It was scary—and also impressive—like nothing was ever out of his control.

"Did you see the dessert bar?" Jake's mom said, trying to change the subject. "There's, like, thirty different flavors of macaroon."

Jake, who had been quietly judging the dinner up to now, saw Nathaniel standing tall across the room. He was wearing a tailored black suit with a black shirt, like he was going to a celebrity funeral. After speaking briefly with the hostess, he headed toward the table, carrying himself with an elegance that clashed disorientingly with the image of him that the headmaster of the Roderick

School had painted in the letter that had arrived that afternoon. When he reached the table, he stood silently, ramrod straight, with his hands on the back of his chair, that wry smirk Jake knew so well plastered on his face.

Cameron smiled to himself, lost in thought. He was so consumed by his mood that he didn't notice that Nathaniel had arrived.

"I could get us a platter," Jake's mom said. She hadn't noticed Nathaniel's presence, either. "To share."

Cameron tilted toward her until his shoulder touched hers. He smiled, letting her kindness soften him for a second. "I'm not in the mood for sweets, love," he said. "I'll take the tart. But by all means, get some for yourself. Fill your purse up for later."

Jake wondered, with a mixture of concern and hope, how long she'd be able to affect Cameron like this. He seemed to be able to turn his affection on and off.

Finally, Jake's mom realized Nathaniel was there. She patted Cameron's chest, a gesture that was both calming and loving, and said, "Hi, Nate. Merry Christmas."

A second later, in a delayed reaction, Cameron turned toward Nathaniel himself. "The man of the hour," he said acidly. "Sit. Eat. Gorge yourself. You should get it while you can, 'cause we're almost ready to leave."

Nathaniel just smiled and took his seat.

For the next half hour, while Jake and his mother nibbled at the desserts she had piled onto a plate for the table, it felt like they'd all fallen into the Twilight Zone. Nobody talked about the news from the Roderick School even though they all felt its chilly shadow. Instead they listened to Jake's mom fill up the time with a long-winded description of the lengths she'd gone to in order to ensure that Tiki Tiki Java had authentic, locally sourced eggnog for the holidays. Cameron seemed quietly pleased to let her carry the conversation. Nathaniel just smiled his cryptic smile, not saying a word, and Jake couldn't help feeling like he was the target of that smile. Every time he glanced in Nathaniel's direction, he felt like he was looking at one of those paintings where the eyes weirdly follow you around the room.

"Okay, time to go," Cameron finally, abruptly said.

Outside, he handed the valet a set of keys, and a couple minutes later, the guy returned, not with the Lexus they'd arrived in but with a black Mini with a checkerboard hood. He held the door open for Cameron to enter, but Cameron backed off. He placed a hand on each of Jake's shoulders.

"Merry Christmas," he said.

It took Jake a second to realize what he meant.

"Go ahead. Drive it home."

Jake glanced at his mother, who beamed at him—she'd been in on the plan and Jake could see all over her face how proud she was to have been able to facilitate his getting something she knew he'd always wanted. Jake looked to the heavens, trying to control his excitement.

"Nice," said Nathaniel coolly. "Good to see we're all getting such killer presents this year."

Cameron nodded, not looking at him. "Don't push it, Nate. Your present is getting me to clean up your mess one more time so you can graduate from high school."

Not even this rattled Nathaniel, though. He just went on smiling as though nothing in the world could ever touch him.

Jake could feel himself blushing in embarrassment. "Thanks," he said to his mom.

"Don't thank me, thank Cameron," she said. "I just told him what you might like."

"Thanks, Cameron," he said.

He wasn't sure what to make of the gift. It was definitely the most extravagant thing he'd ever been given, and it was true that he'd been dreaming of owning a Mini since before he got his driver's license, but something about the way Cameron was displaying his favoritism so blatantly like this made Jake uncomfortable. He couldn't help but feel like Cameron had an ulterior motive, as though he was using Jake to get back at Nathaniel somehow. He hoped not. From what he'd learned so far, that was a mess he wanted nothing to do with.

Cameron patted his shoulder. "You deserve the best," he said.

Jake had to say something, so he told Cameron, "I

can barely believe this is actually happening."

"Oh, it's happening," Cameron said with a chuckle. "You're in the big leagues now."

Jake knew better than to check Nathaniel's reaction.

He climbed in his new car and tooled out of the parking lot.

It wasn't until he was out of the long, winding driveway and off the peninsula, back on the shore road, heading home through the bright gaudy tunnel of decorations the city had strung through downtown for the holidays, that he fingered the guitar pick hanging from his neck, realizing that if Cameron thought he was the big leagues, he must mean Jake's dad was the minors.

Bastard. Jake was starting to see where Nathaniel got it from.

LAUNDRY DAY

Electra is spinning. *She bounces around like a satellite circling some point of gravity, her arms and legs flailing, ping-ponging, sometimes twirling in circles. She floats in darkness, spinning and spinning and spinning and spinning, growing smaller with each turn around the circle.*

We're pulling away from her. She's growing smaller. We move through a pane of glass, the window of a dryer. And Electra's trapped inside. We're in a Laundromat—bright fluorescent lights, crisp rows of machines.

She's spinning faster now.

Faster.

Faster.

The dryer begins shaking, rattling. A crack forms and grows until the dryer has split in half.

Out steps Electra.

She tries to march out of the Laundromat, but she's chained to the wreckage of the dryer. Pulling it behind her, one jerking drag of her leg at a time, she makes her way to the front door. A thick, wide man in a guayabera shirt and fedora stalks after her, hands on hips. He's joined by a posse of Laundromat employees. They shake their fingers admonishingly.

But she makes it to the door and she's almost out, though the dryer is still dragging her down.

And peeking outside, she realizes the Laundromat employees weren't after her, they were after the gang of faux hawked, tattooed thugs gathered out front. The thugs block her way out. They carry bats and chains and crow-bars and buzz saws. They're jumping up and down and swinging their weapons around.

Electra's trapped between them and employees. She calls out for help from a fat girl wearing a pink sweatsuit, but the girl just laughs and sucks down a Big Gulp, throwing the empty container at Electra's head.

She's being overwhelmed, overrun, disappearing under a mountain of bodies. They pile over her. They pile over one another. They battle one another and she's the one who gets hit.

Cracks appear in her skin every time she gets hit. Light

shoots out of the cracks. With each elbow to the gut or flailing punch to the head, another part of Electra glows hot white. Parts of her begin to fall off. The chain holding her to the dryer shatters. She's a glowing ball of light, growing brighter and brighter.

And brighter.

And brighter.

Until she suddenly kicks her legs and swings her arms and sends the whole pile of thugs and Laundromat workers flying.

In the space that's opened up around her, Electra begins to dance an aggressive salsa. Shooting off sparks, she dances up a pathway, also made of light, that rises from the earth and weaves over the town, into the clouds, and out of the atmosphere. She dances among the stars.

The image gradually washes out into a field of white and these words appear on the screen:

Where are we going?

Anywhere. Everywhere.

Out past the end of the public beach, where the grasses grew to five feet tall and dunes rose and tumbled toward the shore, the land looked, if you squinted, like it must have looked four hundred years ago, when the deer and the lizards ruled the beach. If you knew where to look you could find a footpath through the grass that would take you to an old, dilapidated pier, bleached by the sun, rotting in spots, shooting into the water, then breaking where the central portion of pier had collapsed, and then, farther out, rising up again, a wooden island propped above the waves.

Jake and Elena had come here every Christmas since they'd first discovered the place when they were twelve.

It was their secret place, a magical spot that they sometimes felt like they'd invented themselves just so no one could find them.

On Christmas afternoon, Jake sat on the last slats of pier, dangling his feet off the edge and studying the way the shore line curved out before him, trying not to think about the possibility that Elena was standing him up. He'd been there for twenty minutes already and still there was no sign of her.

He knew he shouldn't worry. He was early and there were still ten more minutes to go before the time they'd agreed upon to meet. He couldn't help it, though. He was a ball of unraveling nerves today because what if she saw his gift—his whole heart, that's what he was giving her, his undying love—and didn't want it? What would he do then? How was he supposed to keep going after that? Just the possibility blotted out his ability to think.

He patted his guitar, strummed the strings just once, as though somehow the instrument could calm him down. He checked the time on his phone again. Gazed down the pier, squinting, searching for a rustle in the grass that might imply she was about to appear. Checked his phone again. Kicked himself for arriving early instead of playing it cool and showing up fashionably late.

Five minutes went by. He checked his phone again. Maybe she'd figured out what he had planned and instead of facing his truth, she wasn't coming.

He checked his phone again.

He was almost ready to give up when he saw a flash of color rising over the dunes. Could it, was it . . . Yes. It was her. Wearing a sun hat and a ribbed white tank top, her tight faded jeans distressed and torn in numerous places, Elena trudged through the sand toward him. God, was she beautiful today. More beautiful than he'd ever seen her. She seemed to glisten, to glow, in the light.

Cymbals crashed in his ears. It was going to happen. She'd finally know how much he loved her and why he'd been acting so weird lately. He couldn't back out now. Well, he could, but he wouldn't.

"Hey," she said when she reached the pier. "You been here long?"

"No," he lied. "Just got here."

"I saw the Rumbler parked up there and wondered if I had the time wrong."

He'd left the Mini at home. He wasn't ready to really drive it yet, not in his everyday life. To do so felt too much like a declaration, like he'd be saying, *Yes, now I'm Cameron's son.*

"Naw," he said. "I was actually a little early." He stood up and pulled his Ray-Bans off his eyes, propping them on in his hair. "Merry Christmas," he said.

She made a funny face, crossing her eyes momentarily and sticking out her tongue. "Ho, ho, ho," she said. Then, more seriously, "Merry Christmas, Jake."

When he held his arms out to hug her, she rushed right in and held him tight. He felt her ribs under her tank top. He felt her forehead pressed into his chest. Her body heat rubbing up against his. And he knew this was either the last time they'd ever hug or the beginning of a whole new world for them.

She excised herself from his arms and pulled back, gazing around at their secret place. "Here we are again," she said. "Another Christmas and the pier hasn't rotted away."

He smiled awkwardly. "Yeah."

She must have sensed that his mood needed an injection of excitement, because she plopped down on the pier and began digging in her backpack. "It feels like it's been forever and I'm expecting a full report, every single detail of what you've been up to since we talked, but first—presents!" She held up a small rectangular box wrapped, ironically, in Kwanzaa paper.

Jake settled across from her, cozying up as close as he could without invading her space. He knew exactly where their knees might inadvertently touch and he both wanted it and was afraid of it happening.

He opened her present carefully, not ripping the paper. The box was made of black leather, with a silver latch. Inside was a green frosted sea glass finger slide. He held it up to the sky and peered through it, turning it in the light. "Wow," he said. "Where'd you find this?"

"A girl never tells," she said.

He studied it some more. "It's sort of perfect," he said.

He pulled the thumb drive on which he'd burned new versions of all his songs—replacing Sarah, the fake name he'd used in them, with Elena, the name he'd heard in his head when he'd written them—out of his back pocket and twirled it in his fingers. This was the moment of truth. Once she listened to the songs, she'd know how he felt, even if he didn't tell her today.

"Jake?" she said. "You still here?"

"I . . . Yeah." He handed her the thumb drive. "Sorry. My usual masterful wrapping job."

"A thumb drive," she said, flicking it open and shut. "Just what I've always wanted."

This was the moment. He could tell she was waiting for an explanation. He could feel his nerves splintering under his skin. His heartbeat sluiced in his ears. For a second he wished he could dive into the water and swim away and never return. But he'd come too far to back out now.

"So, okay," he said, pointing at the thumb drive. "That's a compilation of all my songs. Like, the demo versions. The *real* versions. You'll see. They're different from the ones I play in public. But first . . . I'm an asshole."

"Well, we all know that," she teased.

He smiled in recognition of her joke and tried not to

let it rattle him. "That stunt I pulled at Tiki Tiki Java. It was just . . . That's not what I had planned. I was upset. And I'd gotten some crazy-bad advice."

"Let's not talk about that," she said. "It's over. It's done."

"But it's not over. I need to explain. I'd been planning on playing a song for you, just not that song. I'd been . . . and then . . ." He could sense himself getting lost in his words. "You know what, it'll make more sense if I just play it."

He picked up his guitar and cradled it in his lap, then, making a show if it, slipped the slide she'd given him over his finger.

"So, this is called 'Driftwood.' I wrote it for you," he said. He strummed the guitar a couple of times, psyching himself up. Then he began to play.

Don't hate me for loving you
Oh-o'delay
Don't let the sea wash me away

Throughout the first verse, he kept his gaze fixed on his fingers as he played, not because he needed to watch them in order to get through the song but because it was safer to do this than to see Elena's expression. He could feel her listening and as he reached the chorus, his voice cracked. He tried to pretend she wasn't there—or that wasn't exactly it: he tried to pretend that the possibility of her rejection wasn't there, to imagine that she already knew how much he loved her and that she'd already embraced everything that meant. But it wasn't that easy.

He closed his eyes and reminded himself to think of the song, to become one with it, and as he continued through the next couple verses, his connection with the music grew stronger. He threw every ounce of his being into the song. This was the performance of his life. He knew he had to make it good.

Strumming out the final fadeaway, he could feel himself exiting the dream.

He looked up at her. She had tears in her eyes. Maybe this was a good sign.

He reached out and took her two hands in his, held them lightly, thrilling at the feeling of her skin against his.

"They're all for you," he said. "They've always all been for you. There is no Sarah. No girlfriend in the Keys. There's just . . . you. Elena . . ." He could see she was struggling to keep herself from sobbing. But she hadn't pulled her hands away and she hadn't told him to stop, so he pushed on. "I love you. I always have."

Then, not knowing what else to say, he fell silent and gazed into her dark eyes. He'd revealed everything. He was totally exposed. Now it was up to her to decide what to do with him. If only she'd stop crying.

"Oh, Jake," she said finally, wiping her cheek with the back of her arm. "Oh, my sweet Jake."

And just like that he knew he'd made a mistake.

She patted his hands and let them go, but she kept her eyes locked with his, gazing deep into his soul.

Was that pity in her eyes? Why didn't she say something? This waiting for a response was excruciating. He wished he could just disappear.

"I'm sorry. This was a stupid idea," he said, trying to grab his dignity back.

"Don't say that, Jake," she said. She wiped more tears from her cheek. "It's not stupid."

"Does that mean you love me back?"

She tried to smile at him. "I don't know what to say. I mean, Jake, of course I love you. I adore you. But . . ." She took a deep breath and he could tell she was searching for the words that would allow her to let him down easy.

"'But,'" he said. "That's great. That's terrific."

"I didn't mean it like that," she said.

"How did you mean it, then?"

"Jake, you're my best friend. You mean more to me than anyone in the world. I don't want to . . ." Her eyes pled with him, asking him not to make her say it. It was like she wanted him to think this hurt her more than it hurt him. "Remember all those conversations we had when we started high school? About how sex changes things? How love can come and go, but friendship is forever?"

"Yeah," Jake said. "So?"

"So, I don't want to mess it up."

"I don't want to mess it up, either," he said. "I can't help how I feel, though."

She furrowed her brow, thinking about this. "I don't know what to say," she said again.

"You don't mean that," he said. "What you mean is you're afraid to tell me that you don't love me back."

She sat there, a tragically sad expression on her face, and said nothing.

He couldn't bear to hear any more. He couldn't bear any of this. *What a fool. What a total fool.* That's all he kept thinking. Slinging his guitar over his shoulder, he climbed to his feet. "I gotta go. I'm sorry."

"Jake, please don't go," she said.

Then he was race-walking away. He could hear her calling after him, "Wait, Jake. Don't just leave like this," but he didn't dare turn to look at her or slow his pace. His heart felt like it had shattered in his chest. A million achy shards, each one causing its own pain.

Worst Christmas ever. Those are the words that went through Elena's mind, over and over again, as she stood on the grass at the edge of the lawn watching the police wrangle Matty down the front walkway and into their cruiser. First Jake—poor Jake—had proclaimed his love for her and she'd inadvertently broken his heart. Now this.

Her father was there, too, fists on hips, his usually perfectly greased-back hair hanging in wet spikes down over his forehead. He shouted an unending string of curses at Matty in Spanish, punctuating them every once in a while with an accusatory jab of his finger toward the cop car. "How dare you!" he shouted. "How dare you steal from me! You think I don't notice what's going on in my own house?!"

She should have seen it coming. This morning, before she'd skipped out to see Jake, she'd noticed that her father had been brooding like a king, growing brittler and barkier by the hour. Three or four days were about as long as Matty could last before everyone got fed up and wanted him gone. Whatever he'd done this time, she was sure, he deserved this.

The saddest part was that Nina's clothes and hair products and personal accessories were strewn all over the lawn and she herself was slumped on the concrete lip of the porch, sobbing her eyes out. Elena didn't have to be told what must have gone down—she didn't *want* to be told; it was too depressing. Nina pleading with her father, pulling on his arm, begging, lying about how Matty would make it up to him, maybe even claiming that it was her who'd been stealing. Her father looking at his pregnant daughter and giving her an ultimatum. *Either stop covering for him, stop enabling him, or you can leave with him. It's your choice.*

And Nina, being Nina, rising to the bait because no one, not even her father, got to speak to her like that without a fight. Then the inevitable moment when Dad goes to slap her and, seeing her pregnant belly, stops himself in horror. Everyone jumping and banging around the house like firecrackers, popping off in a cacophony of noise. Dad ripping the drawers out of Nina's dresser and dumping her stuff out the front door.

Worst Christmas ever. No doubt about it.

Elena couldn't help but wish that Jake could see this scene with Matty and Nina, this constant craziness and resentment, everyone yelling all the time, unable to control their passions, unable to stop themselves from hurting one another. Maybe then he'd understand why she couldn't seriously consider him romantically. She knew she could be as hotheaded as the rest of the Rios family. Why would she ever want to subject him to this?

She tried to make herself small. She crouched under the magnolia tree at the edge of the property and hoped they didn't see her. But inevitably, they would, no doubt about that.

Crawling away, she darted around the bush that marked the edge of old Mrs. Rodriguez's property and then she popped up and raced down the block.

On another day, Elena would have called Jake. But she couldn't do that. She didn't want to do that. It would be cruel. It would be like she was rubbing his face in it somehow.

She dialed the number she had for Harlow. It didn't even ring. Straight to an electronic auto-message. "The caller you are trying to reach is unavailable at this time."

It figured.

His words from yesterday echoed in her head. "Where

are we going?" she'd asked. And he'd responded, "Any-where. Everywhere." *Yes, Harlow,* she thought. *That's a great idea. Let's run away.*

Race-walking up the street, barely looking where she was going, she checked her AnAmerica account on her phone. Maybe she could reach him that way.

One new message. It was from Harlow. Just the sight of his flaming motorcycle glyph evoked the thrilling sting where he'd bitten her lip.

"Hey, babe, sorry I had to jet like that yesterday."

"It's cool. Shit happens," she wrote. "Is everything okay?"

"Nothing I can't handle. You miss me yet?"

"I was just thinking about you, actually," she responded. Then, because she needed someone to tell her she was good, she typed, "And you? Do you miss me?"

"Sure."

He was playing it cool. Or maybe he just *was* cool. But she'd take what she could get from him right now.

"I think we've got some unfinished business, yeah?"

"Definitely," she typed. Then she added, "My lip still hurts."

"Good pain or bad pain?"

She imagined Harlow's voice whispering in her ear and a flash of heat rushed up her neck. It felt slightly dangerous. It scared her a little.

But not enough to make her stop wanting him.

"Good pain."

Romance was a treacherous game. All the more proof she could never get involved with Jake.

Another message came in from Harlow. "You around New Year's Eve? Wanna go to a party?"

"Maybe."

This seemed like a good place to break it off. She slid her phone into her pocket, abruptly ending the conversation with Harlow, thinking, *Two can play this game of cat and mouse.*

Plopping down cross-legged on the grass, Elena watched the colored lights strung around the archway over the door of the house on the corner blink on and off and on and off and on and off. Jake's song floated through her head. The one he'd written for her. It really was a beautiful song.

She thought about how vulnerable his face had looked as he'd sung it and she felt guilty about the way she was drawn to Harlow. It didn't seem fair. She hadn't chosen to feel the sparks with him. It had just happened. And she couldn't help resenting Jake for putting her in a situation now where just by being herself she'd inadvertently become the kind of callous, soulless, selfish girl that the two of them had always hated.

Even as he knocked on Arnold Chan's bright red front door, being careful not to jar the wreath that had been loosely mounted on it, Jake told himself he shouldn't be doing this.

He'd been bouncing back and forth between deep, drowning sadness and a frantic anger—at himself, at Elena, at Harlow, who, he'd decided, must be the real reason Elena had rejected him.

He knew this was crazy. He knew that the situation was much more complicated than Elena just liking some other guy. But he had to blame someone and he couldn't blame himself and to blame Elena hurt his heart too much. So why not blame Harlow? The guy—or whoever it was catfishing Elena—wan't just hurting her. He was hurting Jake, too, now.

His adrenaline rushed like a waterfall. One word and only one word reverberated in his skull. *Harlow. Harlow. Fucking Harlow. Harlowharlowharlow.* How dare this guy take his Elena away from him?

He heard shuffling inside. Then the door opened a crack, pulling against the chain lock, and Arnold peered out at him under his side-parted hair with one bleary eye.

"Jake!"

Arnold shut the door again and unlatched it. Then, throwing the door wide, he gazed out at Jake with an overeager smile.

"I can't believe you're here. Wow." Arnold's expression went vacant, like he was starstruck. Then he said, "Wow. You want to play Xbox?"

Even though it was winter break, he'd covered his doughy body with his usual uniform of pleated tan pants, gray polo shirt, and rumpled Windbreaker, the same exact thing he wore every single day.

"I need your help, Arnold," Jake said, struggling to play it cool. He was conscious of the fact that Arnold fell somewhere mildly on the autistic scale and he didn't want to upset or overly excite him. He knew from experience not to make any promises he couldn't keep. To do so risked confusing and agitating the kid.

"Okay," Arnold responded, much too quickly.

"Do you want to know what it is first?"

Arnold thought about this for a second. "Yeah. I should know what it is, shouldn't I? But I want to help you, Jake. How cool would it be to be able to help you?"

"Well, first, how about we go inside."

"Oh. Yeah. Good idea."

Arnold stepped back from the stoop and let Jake enter the meticulously tasteful foyer with its pale-blue-and-yellow striped wallpaper, its polished mahogany table and antique mirror, like an imitation of a Victorian drawing room.

"Are your parents home?" Jake asked.

"Yeah."

Jake glanced up the stairs and into the fully dressed dining room, seeing no one. Still, he didn't want Arnold's parents to know what he was up to, so he said, "Should we go somewhere private?"

"We can go to my lair," Arnold said.

He led Jake down the carpeted stairs to the basement, and then through the unfinished space to a dark room at the back where he'd set up his electronic command center. There were three computer screens lined up side by side. On one, Arnold was streaming a Civilization V mod. On the next his Second Life avatar appeared to be sleeping. On the third, he'd been playing some sort of medieval strategy game with a timer saying he had

8.4 hours to wait before his next move. They sat down on the metal folding chairs in front of these screens, and Arnold, still awkwardly eager, still a little too pliant, gazed at Jake, waiting to be told what to do.

Jake took a deep breath. He felt weird using Arnold's adoration like this. The guy had a hard time of it. He'd had his one moment of notoriety, after inadvertently being responsible for projecting that Jules Turnbull sex tape at graduation last year. For a while people had made fun of him for this, until they went back to ignoring his existence, and Jake had always felt distantly protective of him. But he didn't know anybody else who could possibly help him.

"So," he said. "We might be breaking the law a little bit. You know how to hack?"

"I think so," Arnold said shakily.

"I need you to find out everything there is to know about somebody. Anything incriminating. Anything I can use against him."

"Why?"

"I can't tell you."

"Oh," Arnold said, not challenging Jake any further.

"He lives in Dream Point," Jake said. "Or near Dream Point, anyway. Driving distance. His name is Harlow. I don't know his last name. And he hangs out sometimes on the website AnAmerica. Is that enough to go on? Can you help me?"

Arnold's brow pinched slightly for a moment and he glanced at his various computer screens. Jake wasn't sure if he was concerned about doing something illegal or about letting him down. He reminded himself that Arnold's greatest pride was his external hard drive full of stolen movies.

"Arnold?" he said, feeling like an asshole. "I really need the help. I'll owe you a huge favor."

Arnold blushed and rushed his words. "Will you write a song about me?"

"Uh, sure," said Jake.

"Wow," Arnold said. "Wow. Okay. Wow." He furrowed his brow, and then, in that abrupt, awkward way that always sounded nervously half-rehearsed to Jake, he said, "I can track down this Harlow character for you. He must have done some very bad things to get on *your* wrong side. We'll track him down and hunt him like the dog that he is."

25

Ever since Harlow had picked her up, Elena had been feeling surges of light-headedness, like she'd drunk too much champagne or floated too high into thin air. She felt it speeding around the corner as they raced away from her house on the motorcycle. She felt it at the stoplight on Pelican, where he'd twisted back and given her a peck on the cheek. She'd felt it the one time she'd dared to loosen her grip on his waist enough to lean back and gaze up at the stars streaming past above them. It wasn't that she was drunk—she was stone-cold sober—more like, she was overwhelmed by the heady fact that this day she'd been dreaming of for a whole week now had finally arrived.

She felt it again now, as they rolled into the packed parking lot of StarFish, the newest, coolest hotel on the strip. The slick, black facade of the hotel glowed purple and green from the artful night lighting. The place seemed like a magical palace, like everyone who set foot inside would be transformed into a refined, sophisticated, infinitely more interesting person than they'd been before they arrived.

"I feel like I'm in a movie," she said as she stood on the tarmac of the parking lot and waited for her legs to adjust to being on solid ground. "Like I've been taken from my life into some other one where everything is ritzier and more elegant."

"It's not Paris," Harlow said, "but it's the best I could do on short notice."

He held the crook of his arm out for her and she slipped her hand through.

Harlow was wearing a tailored midnight-blue suit that, with his slicked-back wavy hair and his vintage skinny tie, made him look like a 1950s movie star. Elena hoped the festively printed cocktail dress she'd chosen (it had belonged to her mother) held up next to his outfit.

As they headed toward the glass front doors of the hotel, she tried to play it cool, but it was hard to do in the heels she was wearing instead of her usual Doc Martens. She feared she might be outclassed, not just by him, but by everyone else who'd be thronging StarFish's second-floor dance club, SeaHorse, for the New Year's Eve party tonight.

Harlow must have noticed because just as they reached the curb that led up to the entrance, he leaned over and said, "Don't worry. The other girls here are all going to be wishing they were you. You're beautiful. You'll see."

She slipped her hand down Harlow's arm and laced her fingers through his. It might not be as classy as walking arm in arm, but it was more comforting.

They wandered through the frosted glass doors and into the lobby with its plush dark carpet and its industrial steel-and-chrome details, heading straight toward the staircase leading up to the club. She felt like she was in a movie populated with people who were all hipper than she was. The one person she recognized was the concierge: a guy named Peter Talbot whom she remembered having starred in school plays when she was a sophomore. Instead of the Justin Bieber cut he used to have, he'd let his lax bleach-blond hair grow down to his shoulders and he looked different than he used to, older, more cosmopolitan somehow, like someone who knew how important he was.

He went by in a blur and then she and Harlow were inside the dance club, gyrating and popping alongside what seemed like a thousand other people to the pounding beat of the music. Harlow moved like a dream, with none of the awkward hopping and flailing she expected from guys. He had footwork, and as she twirled and swayed, she felt charged by the way his body seemed to anticipate and respond to her movements. She entered an altered state in which the world seemed to disappear and all that existed was his physical presence interacting with hers: the way he kicked his leg, the way he turned his head, the way he found the soft spot at the base of her spine and held one finger there like an acupuncture needle. It was all so intimate and yet so public, like they were inventing a secret language together, a code that contained all their deepest secrets.

Harlow leaned in after a while and shouted something in her ear, but the music was so loud she had no idea what it was. He grinned at her. He winked.

She just smiled and nodded, pretending to understand.

Taking her hand, he led her through the throngs and out into the lobby. She saw from the clocks on the wall behind the check-in desk that an hour and a half had passed, though it had felt like ten minutes tops while it was happening. It was eleven already. The new year was only one hour away.

"You want to go on an adventure?" Harlow whispered in her ear.

He led her through the lobby toward the elevators and pushed the up button.

"Tell me you didn't get a room," she said.

"Ha. I can do better than that," he responded. His lip twisted mischievously. "I've just got something to show you. I think you're going to like it."

"What is it?"

"Can't tell."

They stepped into the elevator and he pushed the button for the top floor.

She wanted to tell him she wasn't the kind of girl who just went along wherever the guy told her to go. But she didn't know how to say this right now because she *did* want to go wherever he was taking her. She *did* like the thrill of not knowing what he'd do next.

They stood silently side by side watching their reflections in the mirrored door as the elevator rose to the top of the hotel.

When they exited, he put a finger to his lips and motioned for her to take her shoes off. They tiptoed down the velvet-lined hallway, past the two suites that occupied the entire floor. Then he opened a door in the wallpaper—she hadn't even realized it was there!—and escorted her into a hidden stairway. Motioning her to follow him, he made his way up the stairs—one flight, two flights. She wondered how he knew about this place, how he could navigate through its secret hidden areas so easily.

"Are we allowed to be here?" she whispered.

He shot her that grin again, not answering, and climbed another flight of stairs. Finally, they reached a door with an emergency exit bar across it. Harlow took out a silver flask and twisted the cap off. He downed a swig and held it out to her.

"Fortification," he whispered.

She took a small tug off the flask and the vodka inside burned in her throat.

Harlow untwisted a paper clip and slid one end into the lock on the door, turning and jiggling it until the door opened.

"You ready?" he said.

The mystery of the moment and the trust she had to place in him thrilled her.

"I'm ready."

He pushed the door open and the brisk air hit their faces and Elena could see that they were at the tippy top of the hotel, standing at the edge of a helipad. The lights of Dream Point spread in a fan around one side of them, and on the other side she saw the darkness of the ocean. She'd never been up so high, and the mixture of romance and transgression contained in the moment brought that feeling of light-headedness she'd had earlier in the evening rushing back.

"Happy New Year," Harlow said. He wrapped his arms around her waist. She could feel his finger pressing into her belly button.

A charge ran up her spine like an electric wire had sparked in her. She felt something spinning inside her skin—so this was what a swoon felt like. The only way to quell the feeling was to kiss Harlow.

So that's what she did. She turned and she pulled him as tight to her as she could and she found his lips with her own, running her hands along his back, excited at the feel of his own on her hips, on the side of her rib cage, on the back of her neck—they seemed to softly flow everywhere, across her body.

The kiss went on and on. She wanted it to never stop. And as they kissed, Harlow walked her backward out of the doorway, onto the cement platform of the helipad.

Surges, like waves, crashed inside her. No matter how close she held him, how deeply she kissed him, she couldn't get close enough to him.

They were down on their knees. They were down on their sides. Still kissing. And then their clothes were coming off. It felt inevitable. Like the only thing that could be done. She'd never wanted anyone or anything as much as she wanted Harlow right that minute.

His hands and his lips seemed to know just where to go and what to do. *So this is what it's supposed to feel like,* she thought. The two guys she'd had sex with in her life had both been clumsy, inexperienced, unsure of themselves. She'd thought it had been her fault, like she'd been somehow doing it wrong, but now, here, with

Harlow, she understood, it had been them. Definitely them.

Harlow had his fingers tangled in her hair, and suddenly, without warning, he pulled her head back, hard, twisting her neck.

She gasped.

For a moment, she felt like she'd lost all control, like he might really hurt her, but then he kissed her neck and released her head and she felt the force of his passion tumble over her fear.

Afterward, as they lay naked and curled together on the chilly cement, she remembered what he'd said on the beach that day. "Where are we going? Anywhere. Everywhere." They really were. She felt reckless and free and far away from all the conflicts that filled up her life.

Something in her itched to tell him how hard she was falling for him. To say, *You're like a dream I never dared to dream. I'd do anything for you if only it meant we could stay like this forever.* But she resisted. She was afraid that revealing herself like that would chase him away, and that was a thought she couldn't bear.

So instead, she held him tight and listened to his breathing, slow and even. He seemed lost in thought. Folding her hands on his chest so she could rest her chin in them and gaze at his face, she asked him what he was thinking.

He looked into her eyes for a long moment and she

felt like his soul was spilling into her own. "I was just thinking how you're the only person in the whole world I feel like I can trust," he said.

Her heart ached for him and all the troubles he kept hidden from her. "Yes," she said. "Yes. You can trust me. I promise."

Jake heard the knock on his bedroom door, he was just choosing to ignore it.

In the week since he'd put Arnold on the case, he hadn't heard back from the kid. As his anxiety and wounded pride tightened in his chest, he'd decided in desperation to put his limited researching tools to the task. He'd been holed up inside for hours with the lights off, searching every animation and video site he could think of, typing random search terms into Google just to see what would come up, obsessively refusing to believe that if Harlow was the person he claimed to be there could be no evidence at all of his existence.

"Jake? I'd really like it if you'd let me in, sweetie."

Jake cringed when he heard the word *sweetie*. This was the third time his mom had tried his door tonight. He realized she was worried about how moody he'd been, but really, *sweetie*? He wasn't a five-year-old.

He shouted through the door, "I'm busy!"

Then he returned to his task. Who knew there were so many anime sites in the world? For the past hour he'd been rummaging around on a Japanese site with a name he couldn't pronounce. It seemed to specialize in videos of samurai and ronin. When he'd stumbled on it, his first thought was of that Sigur Rós thing Elena had shown him that day on the beach. Thinking maybe that he could find that video here, he'd been following link after link, not really sure where they would lead him since all the text was written in Japanese, which showed up as wingdings on his computer.

"It's almost ten thirty," his mother called through the door. "If you're going to celebrate New Year's at all, you should think about getting ready."

Wait, what was this? He'd clicked on a dark, brooding video, painted in watercolors. It didn't have a Sigur Rós sound track, but the visuals seemed pretty similar to what he remembered of the animation Elena had shown him. Could it . . . was it . . . ?

"Jake?"

"Give me one second!"

He cued up the animation again and studied it closely. Either the Japanese kid had stolen it from Harlow or Harlow had stolen it from the kid. Everything in him said that Harlow was the one doing the stealing. As the animation reached its end, he saw a small copyright symbol in the corner of the frame. 2002. That's when this was made. Harlow would have been four or five years old. He'd known it. Maybe, sure, he might really be the person he claimed to be, but he was definitely a fraud. *Bastard.*

The question now was what to do with this valuable information. He'd have to be strategic. And sensitive to Elena's emotions. But he had to wonder, given the way she'd reacted when he told her he loved her, if his new knowledge would make any difference between them.

Anyway, he couldn't put his mom off forever. "All clear," he called. "Mom? You can come in."

His door slowly opened and his mom peeked her head into the room like she was checking for danger before entering.

"You okay?" she said, that steady calming look in her eyes. "I would have thought you'd be doing something with Elena tonight."

Jake looked down at his keyboard. "Yeah, well," he said. "Not this year."

Her gaze remained steady, compassionate. She'd always been this way, letting him come to her with his problems when he was ready, not pushing him, but registering, noticing when he was going through something.

"Cameron's put you on the guest list at StarFish," she said. "You could go check it out. It might be fun."

Jake made a face. He couldn't help it. He couldn't help but wonder when Cameron would want something in return for all the free things he kept throwing Jake's way.

His mom moved deeper into the room. She sat on the bed and folded her hands in her lap.

"I know it's hard," she said.

"What's hard?"

"Getting used to all this." She gestured around the room. "Cameron and his lifestyle and the things he can provide."

Jake looked around the room, focusing on anything but her as he tried to understand what she wanted him to say in response to this. Then, maybe because he was already feeling raw because of Harlow, or maybe because of the pressure to blindly adore Cameron that he felt hovering in the house, or the spooky insinuations he'd picked up from Nathaniel, or all of this together, but Jake couldn't stop himself from defensively blurting out, "What does he want from me, anyway?"

"Nothing," his mom said simply.

Jake couldn't give up his skepticism that easily. "Really?"

"Really. He wants you to feel welcome. He wants you to know he understands that loving me means loving you, too."

"But does he love you?"

Jake's mom tipped her head inquisitively. She was cool, unflappable.

"Of course he does," she said. "Why would you ever think that he doesn't?"

"It's just . . . Nathaniel—"

"Nathaniel's troubled," his mom said, cutting him off. "You can't take the things Nathaniel says to heart."

Jake tried not to let his concern show, but his mom noticed everything. She always had.

Changing tactics, she said, "You know, Cameron's spent years struggling with how to do what's best for Nathaniel. He constantly worries about him. Really, Jake. Give him a chance. He's more sensitive than he sometimes seems to be. He hides behind his charm and sometimes he can seem a little presumptuous, probably, but really he's kind. You'll see as he gets more comfortable with you and begins to let down his guard."

She scrunched her eyes at him.

"Okay?" she said.

Jake tentatively nodded.

"It's New Year's Eve," she said. "You should go have fun."

"All right," Jake said. "I'll go. But I'm doing this for you, not for Cameron."

"That's fine," she said. "These things take time." She checked her watch. "You know, you can still get to Star-Fish in time for the countdown."

Shutting the screen of his computer, Jake pulled on his hooded sweatshirt and slipped into his Cons. He decided he'd take the Rumbler, not the Mini. He wasn't ready yet to change his mind completely about Cameron.

He was pretty sure, also, that he wasn't going to be able to find the energy to enjoy himself. That would take an intervention from Elena, and since their sad conversation at Christmas, she'd stayed away from him. He understood why. If he were her he'd stay away from him, too.

Riding the elevator back to the lobby, Elena and Harlow studied their reflections in the mirrored door.

Elena shined with the afterglow of their adventure on the roof. She adjusted her dress so it hung on her hips in the free-spirited way it was supposed to. She fidgeted with her hair, trying to get her curls to fall back into place and re-create the flapper style she'd worked so hard on before going out.

Harlow played with his collar and tugged at his pant leg.

They were conscious of the possibility of the doors opening at any moment and letting in strangers who might figure out what they'd just been up to on the roof.

They were aware of the camera hidden in the corner above them. They tried their best to act like nothing had happened. Two people waiting to exit and go on their way.

But they couldn't help glancing silently at each other in the mirror every few seconds and smirking, shooting knowing looks back and forth, giggling and then tearing their gazes away from each other, their expressions betraying the reckless glee they were feeling about having gotten away with such a crazy stunt.

As the elevator finally bounced to a halt on the lobby level, Harlow reached across the space between them and gave Elena's thumb one quick squeeze. She felt the intoxicating current of his desire shoot through her body one last time.

Then the doors opened and they stepped out into the throngs of party revelers and hotel patrons as though they were completely innocent, just a guy and a girl getting off an elevator.

"Where to now?" she asked.

She heard the answer she wanted him to give, "Anywhere. Everywhere," bop through her head.

Instead, he glanced at his fancy massive watch and said, "It's almost midnight. We could go back into the club. Watch the clock tick down to—" He froze midsentence. "Fuck."

His eyes narrowed and his body tensed up like he'd been struck by lightning. It took Elena a second to catch up with his change of mood. When she did, a spike of fear shot through her.

"What is it?" she asked.

"Nothing," he said. But his body language said it very much was not nothing. He was making himself subtly smaller, ducking and shifting, eyes darting everywhere. His mischievous, wry half smile had been replaced with a tight-lipped anxiousness, a testy expression that frightened her just a little.

"Something's wrong. I can tell. What is it?" she said, trying not to panic, hoping he'd trust her and let her in.

When he just tensed his cheek and said nothing, peering out at her from someplace deep inside himself that seemed like a universe away, she pushed further.

"It's that guy, isn't it?" she said. "The one who texted you. What did you do to him?"

"He thinks I owe him money," Harlow said, mumbling and swallowing his words. "Like, a lot of money."

She glanced around at the people milling in the lobby—middle-aged couples in tuxedos, the crush of fashionistas spilling down the fan of stairs that led to entrance to the club—but they all just looked like variations on the elegant, rich partiers she'd seen earlier in the evening. She didn't know what or who she was looking for. She imagined some seven-foot goon in a black suit, some massive man with fists like hammers. There was no one who looked like that hanging around the hotel.

"Where is he?" she asked, going up on her tiptoes.

When he didn't answer, she turned to look at him, to let him know that they were in it together.

And just as the New Year's bells started chiming and the cheer went up throughout the hotel lobby, she realized with a shock that he was gone.

28

As midnight approached, Jake found himself slouched in one of the surprisingly hard overstuffed black leather club chairs in the lobby of StarFish. In his faded yellow zippered hoodie and T-shirt, he was beyond underdressed. Everyone else there had done themselves up in tuxes or festive, colorful linen suits.

He couldn't bring himself to climb the plush, carpeted steps and enter the club. Just the pounding of the bass, which he could hear from here, threatened to rob him of his soul.

He hated big see-and-be-seen places like this. They made him feel inadequate, forcing him to confront his loner tendencies and the gulf between himself and the kind of shallow, money-obsessed person American commercial culture seemed to want him to be. And he couldn't help but wonder how many more of these sorts of parties he'd have to go to now that his mom was married to Cameron.

If Elena had been there with him, they could have had fun mocking the pretensions of, say, the pushy woman in the expensively tattered dress who kept stomping angrily back and forth from the club to the front door of the hotel so she could dig through her gargantuan purse for yet another Camel Light. But Elena wasn't here, and even if she were, she probably wouldn't want to sit in the corner being snarky with him—she'd be urging him to make the best of it, bopping her head, saying, *We don't have to join them. We can make our own party over here in the corner.*

Trying to make himself inconspicuous, Jake played with his phone, flipping through his songs, and pretended that he wasn't as lonely and heartbroken as he felt. When he heard the dinging of the hotel's piped-in New Year's bells and the shouts of "ten, nine, eight, seven, six" from the mob spilling out of the club, he felt himself slumping lower in his chair, like the countdown was hammering him into a hole. There just didn't seem to be much to celebrate this year.

The shouting in unison continued. "Five, four, three, two, Happy New Year!"

There was clapping. Cheering. Noisemakers churned. Confetti flew. Jake looked up to see couples kissing each other.

And then, as though the world existed just to mock him, he saw Elena across the room. She stood by herself near the edge of the black marble check-in desk, looking around the room like she was lost.

His heart leaped and a silly vision billowed in his brain of her having come to find him, to embrace him and tell him she'd made a mistake. And then his sank because, obviously, that wasn't going to happen. Unlike Jake, she'd dressed for the occasion. Her gauzy dress was bunched to one side so it hung diagonally over her hips. Her tan skin seemed to gleam beneath it. And she'd tamed her hair and folded it down against her head so that it curled provocatively above her ears.

He wondered if she'd seen him. He wasn't sure if he wanted her to. He faked like he was busy with his phone and studied her out of the corner of his eye.

Then when she did a double take, looked his way again and peered, it was too late. If she hadn't seen him before, she saw him now.

Though he didn't feel up to faking it tonight, there was nothing he could do but throw her a little embarrassed wave now that she knew he was there. Though he ached to be near her, he was afraid to actually talk to her tonight.

She pushed the curl of hair behind her ear and headed toward him. Even teetering slightly on her high heels as she maneuvered around the people blocking her way, she looked impossibly beautiful. Then, as she got closer, he noticed that there was something about the expression on her face—a kind of panic, maybe. A fear. Like she was as afraid of talking to him tonight as he was of talking to her.

Jake sat up straight and slipped his phone into his pocket.

"Hey," he said, trying to hard to play it cool and act like nothing had changed between them. "What brings you to this fine establishment tonight?"

"Oh, I don't know," she said, screwing her mouth into a forced smile. "I just stopped in to use the free bathroom, but then"—she gestured around the room—"I figured I'd stay for the twenty-dollars-a-glass champagne." She was trying to break the awkwardness by making a joke—he'd seen her do it a hundred times with Nina—but he didn't have the energy to laugh along tonight.

As the seconds ticked by with neither of them saying anything, he could feel the pressure of her fumbling through her mind for what to say next.

"It's good to see you," he said, to say something.

"Yeah," she said, a touch of sadness seeping through her voice, "it's good to see you, too."

Then they fell into another awkward silence. She

kept peering around the room. What was she searching for? And why did she have that spooked look in her eyes? Jake felt a pang of longing, of loss. There was a time, just last week, when he'd have known without having to ask what was wrong. Now he didn't feel like he had the right to ask.

Sitting down on the huge arm of his chair, she said, "Good to see you dressed up for the occasion."

"I . . . yeah," Jake said, tugging nervously on his sweatshirt's hood string.

He tried to smile at her, to let her know he appreciated her trying to be the same Elena as she'd always been. Though it hurt his heart, it also pleased him.

The problem was, what to say next? "How've you been?" he asked, finally.

"I've been . . . okay. I've been good, actually. Really good." She peered over her shoulder again. "You?" she said, distractedly. She was being weirdly fidgety, anxious in a way that he could tell had nothing to do with him.

"I'm the same," he said. "You came to this fancy party all alone?"

It took her a second to answer this one, but when she did, she said, "Is there something wrong with that?"

She glanced over her shoulder, searching again. Jake knew she was lying. That was what they'd come to—lying to each other to protect their feelings. He should never have told her he loved her.

"You're here alone, too, aren't you?" she said.

"Yeah, I guess. But I had to come. My mother demanded it. Cameron owns this hotel."

She arched an eyebrow.

"You didn't know that? Yeah. It's all his."

"Wow. I had no idea," she said.

Then, neither of them knowing quite what was allowed and what wasn't, they fell into yet another awkward silence. Jake fought the urge to ask her how things were going with Harlow, to ask her if it was Harlow she kept looking around for. He didn't want to know. Well, actually, he desperately did want to know, but only if things were going poorly. One thing he knew for sure was that, whatever else happened in this conversation, he had to make sure not to mention Harlow's animation or what he'd discovered tonight. It would just piss her off. Even if she conceded that the thing was a fake, she'd think he was being a creep, Google-stalking Harlow and trying to shatter her happiness.

She peered over her shoulder again. She toyed with the silver pendant dangling from her neck, glancing around again every two seconds. And that spooked look in her eyes was still there.

"Everything okay?" he asked. He wanted to comfort her and he almost reached out to touch her forearm, but then he thought better of it. She'd misunderstand.

"Yeah."

"You sure? You seem . . . I don't know—"

"I'm fine, Jake. I'm a big girl," she said curtly. "Just thinking about maybe blowing this pop stand."

"I could give you a ride home."

"No. I'm cool."

"You sure?"

"You know how I like to walk."

"It's, like, six miles. You don't even like to go that far on your bike."

She looked him in the eye and sighed. "Jake," she said, half warning, half pitying. "You're really going to make me spell it out?"

He knew she was trying to protect him, but he couldn't help pushing one last time. "I'm just asking," he said. "I mean, the Rumbler's right outside. Why not just let me drive you home?"

The sadness that passed across her face was almost unbearable to see. "You know why," she said. "It wouldn't be a good idea." She pointed toward the platinum-blond guy standing erect at the concierge station. "I'm going to get Peter over there to call me a cab."

So that's how it is, he thought. He felt like he'd just been slapped.

Then, weakly, he said, "Fine, whatever."

He stood and stretched, trying and failing to brush off his disappointment.

"I guess, then, I'll, I don't know, see you around?"

"Yeah," she said. "Happy New Year, Jake." She stood there, awkwardly for a second, then said, "I'm sorry. I really am."

But her being sorry didn't help at all. Jake got out of there as fast as he could and he couldn't help but think that it was funny in a completely not funny way how this night had so quickly gone from depressing to tragic.

Elena didn't know which was more upsetting, Harlow disappearing the way he had or seeing Jake so mopey and alone and knowing there was nothing she could do about it. Deflated and confused and, honestly, sensing that she might spiral into such a distraught state that she'd never be able to find her way out, Elena stepped barefoot out of the cab on West Palm, one of the more run-down side streets behind the renovated and fancy façade of Magnolia Boulevard.

She checked the address her sister had sent her and scanned the numbers on the clapboard row houses that lined the street. When she found number 264, she buzzed the top buzzer and waited. She hoped Nina was home—and awake.

When nobody answered, she stepped back toward the curb and strained to see into the windows of the third floor. The blinds were shut tight.

She buzzed again, jabbing her finger repeatedly at the button. *Come on, Nina,* she thought. *Just this once . . .*

Just as she felt her fear and need begin to overwhelm her, the door made a grinding sound and she pushed it open. The hallway was narrow and completely enwrapped in old dirty linoleum tiles. She smelled something rank, she couldn't tell quite what.

But she climbed the stairs, slowly, in her bare feet, taking one flight at a time, wondering how Nina, with her weight and her pregnant belly, was able to manage the trips up and down. The thought of her sister standing on the landing halfway up, bent over the railing, huffing as she tried to catch her breath, seemed especially tragic tonight. One more thing to add to the list. Couldn't there be at least one thing in the world that didn't end up turning to shit?

When she reached the top floor, she knocked on the triple-locked door and peered into the peephole.

She heard her sister lumber across the room.

"Who's there? You have to move back for me to see you."

"It's me. Elena," she said, stepping back and waving.

She tried to smile, but she could feel the expression sour on her face. She only had to hold it together for two more minutes, she knew this, but she wasn't sure if she could manage even that.

The locks clicked open, a series of mechanical sounds, and then Nina was standing in semidarkness in front of her, a look of concern softening her face.

It was embarrassing, showing up unannounced and desperate like this. Elena tried to make a joke. "Sometimes you just need your big sister," she said.

Nina made a sympathetic frown and held her arms out so Elena could fall into the soft cushion of her body. She hugged her like she wouldn't ever let her go. Elena managed to surprise herself and not cry.

Finally her sister released her and said, "What happened?"

"I don't know," Elena said. "When I try to put it into words it seems stupid."

They entered the apartment and Elena was shocked and disturbed by what she saw. The mess Nina used to make in the living room seemed to have been magnified by a thousand. The floor was littered with pizza boxes and crumpled bags from McDonald's and Taco Bell, empty beer bottles that Elena had to be careful not to fall on, cigarette butts ground into the hardwood floor.

Matty was passed out on his stomach, half falling off a dilapidated couch that looked like it had been recovered from the street. When Elena saw him, her sister made a face as though to say she was exhausted and beaten down by dealing with him.

They made their way to the corner of the room, where there was a chair Nina could sit in and a leaky beanbag for Elena.

"So," said Nina.

"So, I don't even know where to begin," said Elena. "I had a date and it was amazing—like, transforming. And then . . ."

"You're talking about Harlow?"

"Yeah. Harlow."

Nina nodded sagely, as though she contained some secret wisdom that she wasn't ready to divulge.

Elena could feel the emotions welling up inside her again. She felt like she was going to break into a million pieces. She had to do something to push them out, to hold herself together, but she didn't know what. The tears rose in the corners of her eyes. To ward them off, she began talking, babbling, not even knowing what she was saying.

"When I'm with him, I feel, I don't know. Reckless. Fearless. Like nothing in the world can keep up with me. And tonight, it was just . . . You know when you feel out of control but in a good way? It was like that. We went to this fancy party at StarFish and it was so glamorous and I felt like maybe I could be glamorous, too. You know what I mean? Like because I was with Harlow . . ."

Nina filled in the words she couldn't find. "You felt like you could see yourself the way he saw you."

"Yeah," Elena said. "We snuck up onto the roof of the hotel. It felt reckless. Dangerous."

"Thrilling," said Nina.

"And . . ."

"You had sex."

Elena nodded. She fought back the tears. "But then . . . he just disappeared. Like Christmas Eve when we took that ride on his motorcycle. But worse. This time, he was there and then he wasn't. He just left me at this hotel where I didn't know anybody. He left me, Nina. Just like that. Not even a good-bye. Is that right? Is that normal? And there's these guys after him."

"Hold up, what?"

"There's these guys after him. Like, they want to kill him or something. He said they think he owes them money, which, I don't know what that means. Does he really owe them money? Why? Or does he not owe them money but they think he does? Is there some other thing he hasn't told me about that . . . I mean, it's just . . . it's, like . . . he's a total mystery. Maybe he's into some bad shit or something. I wouldn't know. He won't tell me. He won't let me in. It's like he's trying to protect me, or he's trying to protect himself, or he doesn't trust me, or he doesn't like me, or I don't know."

The tears finally broke through. Elena felt a heat releasing inside her body. She began to sob.

"I don't know anything," she blurted. "How can I be so into this guy when I don't know a single thing about him? Jake would say I shouldn't. Jake hates his guts. But that's a whole other thing."

A new wave of sobs broke inside of Elena. Jake's part in all this was more than she could explain. It was more than she could handle. All she could do now was curl up in a ball and wish the pain would go away.

Nina scooted down to sit next to her on the floor. She held her tight, rocking her, petting her head until her sobs melted into a more consistent, less uncontrollable crying.

Elena asked her sister, "Does it have to feel like this? What's wrong with me, Nina? Why didn't you tell me it was all so hard?"

Nina held her head close and rocked her and rocked her. "Oh, baby," she murmured. "Oh, Elena. If I knew the answer to that question, I wouldn't be here with Matty, would I? Do you think I know how to do the right thing? You know? Us Rios girls. We were made this way. Or we ended up this way. Sometimes I wonder, maybe if Mom hadn't . . ."

Then she started crying, too.

Elena knew what Nina would have said if she'd been able to finish her sentence. She would have said, *Maybe if Mom hadn't died.* But she had. And without her, neither of them had really figured out how to be a strong woman like she'd been.

Elena clutched her sister tighter. They rocked back and forth until it was hard to tell who was comforting whom.

30

Later, unable to shake the melancholy that had come over him after seeing Elena, Jake slung his guitar over his back and wandered barefoot down to the private beach attached to the house. He walked slowly out to the water and watched the waves lap at the sand. The cool water rolled over his toes and the moonlight turned everything a haunted silvery color.

He felt so bottomlessly sad that the feeling was almost comforting, like a long-lost friend, rich with memory and possibility. Like life was real and this moment was important. He told himself to remember the feeling. To remember this walk. To use it in his music.

Not wanting the moment to end, he followed the

tide line along the beach. Jake wasn't sure where Cameron's property ended, but the beach went on forever. He enjoyed the way the wet sand gave under his toes, the way it compressed and grew denser as his feet pressed down on it.

Up ahead, he saw a shape in the sand. A boulder of darkness. It wasn't moving.

When he got closer, he saw that it was a person, sitting with legs curled up. He wondered who else could be out here at this hour.

Then, when he was closer still, he saw the blond waves and the posture of the body and realized, with a sinking dread, that it was Nathaniel, staring, as though in a daze, out at the water.

Jake didn't think he'd seen him yet. He considered turning back. But something about that idea felt like defeat. He had just as much right to be on this beach as Nathaniel did.

He wandered on.

Even when Jake was right on top of him, Nathaniel didn't seem to see him. The guy was crying. Or he'd been crying. His eyes were puffy and bloodshot. He'd propped his silver inlaid flask in the sand next to him and Jake wondered how much he'd had to drink tonight. Nate had never seemed the type to drink himself to tears. He was more the wicked, angry drunk.

Despite everything that had happened between

them, Jake sort of felt for the guy. He wanted to believe his mother about Cameron—he trusted her ability to see through to the hearts of other people—but the guy had been so uncompromising with Nathaniel at Christmas and throughout the week things had just gotten worse between them. They'd barely been able to sit in the same room together. It must be hard to feel like you've so profoundly failed your father.

"Hey," he said, a gesture of goodwill.

Nathaniel looked up at him, and it was like he was seeing through him. There was something vacant in his eyes, like wherever he was in his head was more real than being in the world.

Jake noticed now that he had something in his hands. A slip of crumpled paper. Or no. It was an origami swan like the ones Jake had found all over the bedroom. Nate cradled it almost like it was alive, a baby chick in need of warmth and care.

"What's going on?" Jake said. He slid the guitar off his shoulder and plopped down next to Nathaniel. "You okay?"

Nathaniel didn't answer. He twirled the swan between his two forefingers. He pushed his finger against its beak in a gesture that contained more love than Jake had thought Nate capable of. Finally, when he did speak he seemed to be talking to himself more than to Jake.

"My mom made this," he said. "She made one every

day. A single swan. Sometimes out of an envelope. Sometimes out of tissue paper. Each one was a little bit different from the others. She'd hide them around the house and it was my job to find them. If I did I'd get a cookie. It was a game we played. I'd get home from school and while she did her housework or put away the groceries or whatever, I'd search under pillows and behind the bedposts, inside the flower pots, until I found the swan. It was . . ."

He rubbed his eyes. He was crying again.

"That's a sweet memory," Jake said, not knowing how else to respond. When someone was this distraught, he felt, you had to respect the depths of that person's feelings. Even someone so annoying as Nathaniel.

"She died today," Nathaniel said abruptly, wiping his eyes.

"What?"

"Or not today, but today's the anniversary. New Year's Eve. 2008. We were in the Bahamas. Staying at the resort Cameron owns down there. She jumped off the helipad on the roof of the hotel. Fifteen stories. She didn't have a chance."

Jake wasn't sure if he was supposed to gently pat Nathaniel on the back or give him a hug or what. "I didn't know that," he said. "I'm sorry to hear—"

Nathaniel turned on him with a sudden, barely suppressed rage. "Why would you know? Tell me why you would know! It's not like Cameron would have told you about it." His eyes went far away again for a moment, and then he continued spitefully, "Cameron's the reason she's dead."

What an accusation. Cameron was domineering and self-involved, sure. Jake had figured that out, but to drive someone to suicide? It didn't seem possible that this could be true. Whatever his attitude toward Nathaniel, he'd shown nothing but devotion to Jake's mother. Still, Jake didn't want to disrespect Nathaniel's feelings. He tried to project through his body language that he was listening, that he cared in some way.

"You don't think so?" Nathaniel said, as though Jake, through his silence, had accused him of lying. "You think, *Oh, Cameron. He couldn't do something like that. He's so charming. He bought me a car.* But the dude's a total prick. He's got women hidden in every hotel he owns. Every city in the world. He likes them young and spacey. And psychologically damaged. And my mom . . . He might have been married to her, but he treated her like the hired help. Like the maid who lets you take advantage of her because she's afraid of losing her job."

It was like with every new thought, Nathaniel grew angrier at Jake, even though Jake had nothing to do with any of this. Trying to be both diplomatic and compassionate, Jake placed a hand on Nathaniel's shoulder and said, "It must be really hard, man. I don't know what I'd do if I lost my mother that way."

Nathaniel slapped him away with a violent chop to the arm. The rage on his face had curdled into hatred. Jake felt it burning toward him.

"You'll see," he said. "It won't take that long for Cameron to drive your mom insane, too. He does it to everyone. And then what will you have? Nothing. Nada. You'll have jack shit, brother. Don't think Cameron's going to think you're the golden boy once your mom's gone. That trust fund you think you're going to steal out from under me, you can kiss that baby good-bye. It won't go to me, I'll give you that. He'll find some new woman to make promises to. And he'll roll all that money forward to her kid, just like he did from me to you."

Nathaniel had worked himself up into such a lather that he'd inadvertently crushed the origami swan in his fist.

"I'm not your enemy, Nathaniel," said Jake. "You know? I'm not asking for anything from Cameron. I just think it's all very sad. And if I see him behave toward my mom like that, I'll—"

"Why are you still here?" Nathaniel said in response, his top lip curling malevolently. "Did I ask you to sit here and pretend to care? You're not as sensitive as you pretend to be. You know that? You just like the idea of people thinking you are. Go find someone else to smear your pity all over. Go find that hottie of yours with the cute little strawberry mark on her thigh. She probably needs you to cheer her up. Or is she not yours anymore? You fucked that up already, didn't you? Too bad. Would have been nice to have her around when Cameron takes everything away from you."

That was it. Jake had had enough. He'd tried, he'd really tried to be the bigger person and separate his feelings about Nathaniel from the guy's obvious pain. But there was no way he'd let that be an excuse for this abuse.

"Nathaniel," he said, looking the guy dead in the eye, "you don't know anything about Elena. You don't know anything about me. So do yourself a favor and shut the fuck up."

For a second, neither of them said a word. They just stared at each other, calling each other's bluff.

"Or what?" said Nathaniel. "What you gonna do?" He smoldered, his eyes boring through Jake like he'd kill him if he could.

The adrenaline rushed to Jake's head, blotting out all thought.

And before he knew what was happening, Nathaniel had leaped over him, grabbed his guitar, and spun in a circle, holding it out in front of him. He brought it smashing down on the sand, and when it didn't break, he brought it down again. And again and again, kicking up a cloud of sand around him, busting the neck, and then, still not satisfied, shoving his bare foot through the hollow basin of its body.

Turning to Jake, Nathaniel broke out the smirk he'd been hiding all night. "What you gonna do now, brother? Go tell mommy again?"

Jake didn't think. He couldn't think. He didn't know what he was doing, didn't even know what he was trying to do. He could only react.

He leaped at Nathaniel, swinging his fists, but Nathaniel pushed back with a stiff arm, sending Jake down into the sand. Scrambling to his feet, Jake charged again.

Nathaniel lowered his shoulder and, using his forearms as clubs, he shoved Jake back again with an elbow to the jaw.

On his knees in the sand, Jake felt the coppery taste of blood filling his mouth. He jumped to his feet and charged toward Nathaniel like a wild animal, leaping and grabbing him around the waist. They grappled, each of them stretching for leverage, until Nate buckled and went down on his chest in the sand.

Jake spun and straddled Nathaniel's back. He dug both hands into Nathaniel's hair, and he smashed his face against the sand over and over again, just like Nate had done to his guitar.

For a second, Jake thought, *My God, I could kill this guy.*

All at once he was horrified with what he was doing. He let Nathaniel go, struggled to his feet, and stumbled back toward the house.

SUPERNOVA

A pulsing, pounding techno beat.

A strobe light illuminates the heavens.

In short bursts of stop action caught in the strobe, a slick red-and-white racing cycle roars across the universe along a ribbon of starlight. It passes stars and planets, weaves through fields of asteroids. As it dodges and turns, it throws up sparks, leaving a trail of flames in its wake.

The motorcycle jumps over the moon. Landing hard on the trail of starlight, it wobbles but doesn't fall.

It roars on.

As it gets closer, we can see a stylized Harlow hunched over the handlebars. He wears aerodynamic shades and his full leather gear. His hair is a mess of wavy blond spikes. Behind him, holding on for dear life, sits Electra. She smiles maniacally, with a bright joy that glows all over her body.

Harlow skids to a stop. He reaches into the breast pocket of his leather jacket and pulls out a silver flask inlaid with an image of a stalking tiger carved in ivory. Twisting the cap off, he takes a swig and hands it to Electra. She takes a swig of her own and hands it back to Harlow. He puts the flask back in his pocket and pulls Electra in for a kiss.

Stars explode around them.

Then he opens the throttle and the cycle races onward.

Harlow points to something up ahead. The sun. They're headed right for it. It looms larger and larger.

And suddenly, it's right in front of them, glowing orange, yellow, white hot. Harlow doesn't slow down. He digs in lower over his handlebars and guns it.

Electra, seeing what's about to happen, grapples with him, attempting to peel his hands off the bike, to save them both, but he's too strong, too determined. He shakes her off.

She goes flying, and as she floats away, spinning in the cold cold gravity-less void of space, he surges forward straight into the sun. Sparks and leaping flames and for a moment, he and the cycle can be seen burning up, a singed black silhouette of what they once were.

Then Harlow is gone.

Electra lets loose a silent scream as she floats off into the black nothingness.

32

In the three days since New Year's, Jake had hardly left the house. He'd hardly even left his room. Lurking around in the gloomy darkness, he picked at his guitar—his secondary guitar, a crappy old Crescent that fell out of tune every ten minutes—and brooded over all the ways his life had gone wrong since moving with his mother into this ridiculously opulent house.

There was Elena, first, of course, and the sad, swift deterioration of his relationship with her. It used to be that he could intuit what she was thinking just by glancing at her. Now it seemed like he barely knew her. She been so distant when he'd seen her at StarFish, like one of those kids at school who tolerates you but keeps his in-jokes to himself, leaving you to wander away feeling less connected to him than you were when you first said hi. He hadn't heard from her since and he'd been so demoralized by the experience that he hadn't dared reach out to her himself. The whole thing had upset him so much that he couldn't even write a song about it. He just felt sad and confused.

That would have been bad enough, but there was also Nathaniel.

The thing that really got him, the thing that, if he was being honest, had been sticking in his gut and making him sick all week was the way Nathaniel had sneeringly talked about Elena during the argument they'd had on the beach. "Go find that hottie of yours with the cute little strawberry mark on her thigh."

That's what he'd said. Jake would never forget it. And how did he know about Elena's strawberry mark? He'd never seen it. He'd never met Elena.

By the time Jake had worked himself up enough to consider confronting Nathaniel about it, the guy had left town, headed back up to the Roderick School with Cameron to pay them off and get himself reinstated. Cameron was back and he'd left Nathaniel up there, which was a relief, but even so, every time Jake ventured out of his room, it was like he could feel Nathaniel's presence, anyway. His oily sheen, like the trail of a slug, clung to every square inch of the house.

Better to keep himself locked in, out of sight, alone with his wounds and his pride.

But even here, the world came rushing in. He couldn't avoid checking the internet. Especially now that Elena had posted a new video. Electra and Harlow on a motorcycle, racing through the universe.

He'd watched it at least a hundred times, and each time just made his stomach knot tighter. It didn't even matter that the ending implied that there might be some trouble between the two of them. What mattered was the way it sparked and clarified so many associations that Jake had been sensing but not really understanding. A question had begun to form in his mind:

What if Harlow was really Nathaniel?

He watched the video again, now, with a notebook in front of him, pausing it every time he saw something new.

Harlow's spiky blond hair. Pause. He jotted down a note: "Blond Short and Wavy = Nathaniel."

The flask. Pause. "Stalking Tiger = Nathaniel. Is this a coincidence? How many flasks can there be like that?"

Not many. And if there were more of them, how many of them would be owned by a blond guy who lived in Dream Point?

He stopped the video before it got to the part where Electra reaches out to futilely try and save Harlow. He didn't want to see her yearning for someone else. Instead, he cued it up again and studied what he saw.

That crotch-rocket motorcycle. Pause. He'd never seen Nathaniel riding one of those. He wrote, "Cycle. Does Nathaniel have one? Where does he hide it?"

So, one point against, two points for.

He tapped the tip of his pen rapid-fire against the notebook page, trying to think of other relationships he may not have noticed before.

There was that ronin video Harlow had stolen from the Japanese site. Could that have been Nathaniel? Was he savvy enough with editing programs to strip out the sound track and replace it with a new one? Maybe, maybe not. If nothing else, it was proof that Harlow wasn't who he presented himself as being. Best to note it either way. Jake wrote in his notebook, "Ronin? False pretenses? Possible purposeful targeting of Elena? But . . . motive?"

Realizing that there was no way to connect the stolen clip to Nathaniel, Jake backed away from the thought. Too much speculation would lead him down a rabbit hole. But how else to untangle his gut feelings? He doodled in the margins of his notebook. A rabbit peering over a hole. A crappy version of Elena's stylized Harlow character. Then, annoyed both by his lack of drawing talent and the fact that this Harlow was staring up from his notebook, he scribbled it out.

Unless he had, which—yes. He had. He must have. Jake was barely able to get the trash can out from under the desk in time to catch the vomit burning up his throat. He pressed his forehead against the sharp edge of the desk and spit the residual bile out of his mouth.

Harlow. Nathaniel. They were the same person. He knew it. He just knew it. Even if he couldn't prove it.

His mind wandered back to various times Nathaniel had disappeared.

New Year's Eve. He'd run into Jake on the beach, that was true, but where had the guy been earlier in the evening? And was it possible that he had something to do with Elena's weird mood that night? Come to think of it, why would Elena have been at StarFish at all if she hadn't been dragged there by someone like Nathaniel?

And what about Christmas Eve? He knew Elena had seen Harlow—she'd told him about it. Was it possible that this was why Nathaniel was so late for their dinner at The Spanish Armada? Hell yeah, it was possible.

Jake grabbed his cell phone off the bed, where he'd thrown it. He couldn't help noticing that he had no new text messages. No word from Elena. Still. It had been three days now. His imagination flashed on what would happen when they returned to school on Monday. More awkwardness. More rejection. He couldn't bear to think about it.

Anyway, he wasn't about to call her now. He had work to do. He dialed Arnold Chan.

"Jake! Wow! I was just thinking about you," Arnold

said, answering on the first ring.

"Oh? I was thinking about you, too, Arnold."

"We should hang out. Do you like BioShock? I got the new BioShock for Christmas. You should come over. We can play it one-on-one."

"I can't, Arnold. I'm really busy right now."

"Writing new songs." Arnold said this with a kind of dusting of pride.

"Yeah. Exactly," Jake responded. "But, listen, have you made any headway on that thing we discussed? Any idea what the IP address is or where it's located?"

"The dog," Arnold said darkly. "We will hunt him down. We will put an end to his dastardly adventures."

Jake didn't have the energy for Arnold's autistic melodrama right then. "Yeah," he said. "But have you learned anything yet?"

For a long minute, Jake heard nothing but silence.

"I've learned a lot of things," Arnold finally said.

"Like what?"

"It's classified right now."

Jake had had enough. "Arnold. You haven't learned anything, have you? Do you even know how to do this? Be honest with me. I know you don't want to let me down, but I really need this information."

Again, silence on Arnold's end of the line.

"I know how to do it," Arnold said. "You'll see. I'll be your hero. I'll have what you need in thirty-seven and one-quarter hours. I promise."

"I'm counting on you," Jake said, almost pleading, realizing as he said it that he was at Arnold's mercy.

"I'm counting on me, too," Arnold said.

Jake cringed.

But despite Arnold's oddly precise calculation, Jake reflexively glanced at the time as he hung up. Thirty-seven and one-quarter hours would be eight a.m. on Monday. Homeroom. The first day back from winter break.

Through the window, Elena listened as the cab slowed to a stop in front of her house. She watched as the door opened and Nina placed one leg then the other on the sturdy pavement of the street, taking care to ensure that her feet were well planted.

As the driver hefted Nina's small pink roller bag out of the trunk, Nina braced herself on the open door and pulled herself slowly out of the cavern of the backseat. Elena watched her totter up the driveway, dragging her tiny suitcase behind her. The rhinestones spelling out *Juicy* on her sweatpants sparkled in the sun. Her hair hung limp and distressed across her face, but as she got incrementally closer, Elena could see that her face was flushed and puffy, her cheeks streaked black. She'd been crying.

Matty. Damn him.

It must have been bad for Nina to pull herself out of her state of inertia and make the trip home like this. Elena jumped up from the couch, where, with Nina gone for the past ten days, she'd been able to nestle as she sketched out storyboards and experimented with the filters in Final Cut Pro, and prepared herself to be outraged on Nina's behalf.

She threw the door open before Nina had made it halfway up the drive, and, standing on the mosaic portico, hands on hips, she called out to her sister. "What happened? Are you okay?" she asked.

The wounded look reaching out to her from Nina's face broke her heart. She felt her sister's pain like it was her own. And then she felt a vengeful, defensive rage bubble up in her.

"What did he do, Nina?" Elena asked. "Did he hit you? Did he hurt the baby? I'll kill him."

Propping her roller bag back on its wheels, Nina let loose a massive chest-heaving sigh. She looked like she was going to crumple to the pavement, but instead she sat on the top of the bag. And she sobbed.

Elena felt a tug in her chest, an acute ache for her sister's well-being. She ran to Nina. Wrapping her arms around her, she squeezed with all her might.

Pulling herself together, Nina asked, "Is Dad home?"

"He's in the Slats. Colleen called in sick again."

Nina nodded. "Good," she said.

Elena refused to let her go. If only she could hug the pain right out of her. "You gonna tell me what happened?"

"He didn't hit me."

"Well, he must have done something."

"Sabrina Perez. That's what he 'did.'"

"Sabrina Perez?"

"Yeah. That skanky *puta* who hangs out at Cubano Cantina with him and all his jackass *hermanos*." Nina revved herself up to blow her anger and pain into a hot balloon of words. There was the Nina Elena knew. "He wasn't even sorry. He doesn't give a shit. He brought her back to the apartment, and they did the gooney while I was sleeping in the other room! And Sabrina fucking Perez. She was, like, screaming like a dying cat, like Matty—limp-dick, coked-to-the-gills Matty—was the best fuck she'd ever had. Or, really, like she knew if she howled long enough she'd wake me up. She's always wanted him. And she's always hated me because I knew how to treat him. But, ut-uh." She wagged her finger in front of Elena's nose. "Nut-ut-uh! That's all over. She can have him. You know what he said to me? He said, 'What do you expect? It's not like I can get any from you.'"

"God. That's horrible," Elena said.

But Nina wasn't done.

"Then later, when the skank slinks her way out of there, he's begging me to stay. He's all, 'Nina! Nina! I can't live without you!' Fuck him. My baby deserves better than him. I'm moving back in here with you."

Elena's heart froze for a second. She could just imagine the storm that would erupt if her father got home to see she'd let Nina back in. He'd never understand. When he made a decision, he bullheadedly stuck to it regardless of how wrong it turned out to be. If Elena let Nina back in today, it would be just like that time last year when Matty had stolen two hundred dollars from the cigar box her dad kept hidden in his closet. He might just kick both of them out.

"Nina," she pleaded, hedging.

She stepped back to take in the whole of her sister, holding her hand to let her know that she wasn't turning her back on her.

Even so, Nina could see what was coming. "Oh, not you, too," she snapped. "Who's on my side? Where's the person in this whole world who's on my side?"

"I'm on your side. It's just . . . Dad would kill me. He'd kill both of us."

Nina burst into tears again. She hugged her chest like she was showing Elena how hard it was to comfort herself now that she'd let her down. A burbling, bubbling mess of tears. The longer she cried, the more helpless Elena felt.

"Let me talk to him at least. Before you move in. If you can just hold off for a day or two, Nina—"

"And go where? I have no place else to go!"

"Can you go back to the apartment?"

"Matty's there!"

"Well, kick him out. You want me to come with you? I'd kill to tell him off."

Nina looked around helplessly. "My cab's already gone."

"We'll call another one. It's not like they're in demand at four o'clock on a Saturday."

Nina reached out and held Elena's hand. "Please," she said, the tears teetering on her eyelids.

"One day. And I'll talk to Dad for you. I promise."

Relenting, Nina reluctantly nodded. "Okay," she said, sighing.

Elena placed her hand tenderly on Nina's shoulder. "Do you want me to come with you? To deal with Matty?"

Nina shook her head no.

"Okay. You wait here and I'll get you a glass of water. I'll call that cab, too."

As soon as she was back inside, Elena squeezed the bridge of her nose, leaned back against the closed door, and tried to slow her racing mind.

What an impossible situation.

It would take a whole lot of begging to get her dad to change his mind. His pride would have to be massaged. His deeply submerged sense of compassion would have to be slowly coaxed to the surface. She wasn't sure she could succeed if she tried. And Nina, she was all emotion and impulsive action. Without Elena's intervention, they'd barrel into each other like two semis going full speed. And *with* her intervention, she might just get smashed between them.

Mostly, she was afraid that if she tried to intervene, she'd make everything worse. She had a temper, too, and right now it was flaring. It was ironic. If she was going to successfully support Nina, she'd need someone to support *her*.

Whipping her phone out of the back pocket of her black jean shorts, she dialed Harlow. As the phone rang three, four times, she found herself begging him to pick up. He was supposed to be her conquering hero, but she hadn't heard a word from him since New Year's Eve. The phone kept ringing, five, six times, and then it went to voice mail with an automated message: "The caller you are trying to reach is unavailable at this time."

Where could he be? she wondered. Was he really in danger, or had he just flaked? She didn't want to believe that he was the kind of guy to vanish as soon as he'd notched her name on his belt, but part of her worried that maybe he was.

She hung up without leaving a message.

So, what now?

She did the only thing she knew how to do, the thing she'd been doing for as long as she could remember when she felt overwhelmed. She texted her best friend.

"CAN WE TALK?"

It didn't take Jake ten seconds to respond.

"OF COURSE. WHEN?"

"NOW."

As soon as she hit send, she regretted leaning on him like this in her moment of need. It wasn't fair to him. Not when things were such a mess between them. She'd have to be careful, kind, mature. Was she up for it? She hoped so. She needed him. She suspected she always would.

34

It was the magic hour. The thin winter sunlight painted the dunes and the shore road a deep golden ocher. The sea grass rippling in the breeze glimmered like goldenrod.

As Jake drove the Rumbler toward the pier (he still couldn't bring himself to take the Mini out), he could feel the wind in the air ruffle through his hair and he felt like he was entering a movie in which the beauty of the moment draws all the most beautiful possibilities of life. He had to vigilantly stop himself from hoping that Elena had called him here to tell him she'd realized what a fool she'd been, deluded and afraid to admit that she'd loved him all along. That wasn't going to happen. He knew this. But still, he couldn't help fantasizing about her throwing herself into his arms.

He rolled onto the dirt road—really just two wheel tracks through the grass—that led to the dilapidated pier where he and Elena had spent so many lazy afternoons. Her bike was already there, lying on its side. He parked next to it and hiked through the goat trail to the pier, and there she was, like a classical statue, wearing black jean shorts and a tight pink tank top, dangling her legs off the far platform, past the spot where the pier had rotted away.

She was gazing off into space like she was in a trance and she didn't notice him approaching, not even when the wooden slats creaked under his feet, not even when he leaped across the gap to the platform.

Touching her warm bare shoulder, he plopped down next to her.

"Hey," he said. Given how complicated everything was between them, he wasn't sure if he should hug her or not.

Even now, it took her a minute to look up. When, finally, she did, she seemed drained of her usual spunky, protective humor.

"Hi," she said, scrunching up her face apologetically. Then, "Sorry. This is totally unfair. I didn't know who else to call. You're the only one I know how to talk to."

Jake tried to keep his disappointment in check even

though he knew now that she hadn't called him here to profess her love. But seeing her like this, upset, overwhelmed, he cared less about his own feelings than hers. If she was in need, he had to be there for her in whatever way he could. To do any less would be a betrayal of his devotion to her.

"It's okay," he said.

She looked like she was about to cry.

"Elena, it's okay," he said again, more meaningfully this time. He sat down cross-legged across from her. "I'm here. Whatever it is, I'm here. I'll always be here."

Now the tears fell from her eyes. He took her hand and let her cry.

When, finally, she took her hand back and wiped the tears away, he asked, "What happened? Is it Harlow?"

The stricken look that flashed across her face at the mention of Harlow told Jake he'd made a mistake. "Sorry," he said in a rush. "I'm not fishing. I promise. I just . . . Tell me what happened."

After a moment of hesitation in which she seemed to be gauging Jake's ability to comfort her, she rolled her eyes slowly with an ironic sense of resignation, and then she launched into it. "What didn't happen. Matty fucked some girl, and now, well, you know Nina. 'It's all over now,' she says. 'I'm moving back home.' But that can't happen. Dad would kill her. He'd kill me. Tough love, baby. You live with your choices. And anyway, what happens when she decides to forgive Matty? Then we're right back where we started. It's just . . ." She flopped onto her back and gazed up at the clear blue sky. "It's the same old thing over and over again, but somehow it's worse each time. Know what I mean?"

Jake couldn't entirely follow the thread. In the past few weeks, with the strain between him and Elena, he'd missed a few episodes of the soap opera that was Nina's life. It didn't matter. What mattered was that he simply listen and show her he cared.

"Yeah, I know exactly what you mean," he said. "You think she'll ever leave him for good?"

"She claims it's for good this time. But, you know, what fun would that be?" Elena said ruefully.

"Maybe it is. Maybe she's had enough. Maybe it's like my mom back when my dad was drinking. At a certain point, you can't keep sacrificing yourself. No matter how much you love the other person. Maybe Nina's reached that point." He thought for a moment about what might be holding Nina back. "She's probably terrified about raising a baby by herself," he said.

"I'd help her."

"Does she know that?"

"Yes . . . no. Maybe. How could she not?" Elena said.

Jake tipped his head and raised an eyebrow, silently letting her pick up on what he was implying.

"Yeah," she said. "You're right." She gave a little half

laugh. "Like the saying goes, 'When you assume, you make an ass out of you and me.'"

"Exactly," Jake said with a smile. "Baby steps. You'll talk to your dad. You know he can't say no to you. And then you'll see what happens."

Elena let out a sigh. "I've missed you, Jake," she said.

"I've missed you, too."

They stared at each other, embarrassed for a second, then Elena stuck out her tongue and made a funny face. "Anyway," she said, "enough about me. I'm sick of me. What's up with you?"

Jake took a deep breath and thought about what to say and what to keep hidden. "Well," he said, "my, I guess, stepbrother Nathaniel broke my guitar the other night."

"The Gibson?"

"Yeah."

"Oh shit. What did you do?"

"What am I supposed to do? He's . . ." Jake couldn't resist planting a small seed. "You'd see if you met him," he said. "He's a total douche bag. Anyway, he's gone now. Back in Atlanta at the Roderick School, where he would have been kicked out except if they kicked him out they'd lose that nice pipeline of cash they get from Cameron."

She propped herself up on her elbows and gazed out at the water. In the golden light, every curve of her body seemed even more achingly beautiful than usual. "Same shit, different day," she said. Then she made another one of her funny faces.

"Better than a bullet to the head," Jake offered.

"But just barely," said Elena. There was that smile he'd been hoping to see—a little wistful, a little sad, but as gorgeous as ever. "Oh, Jake," she sighed.

Sitting up, Elena scooted closer to Jake and laid her head against his bicep. He was too tall for her to reach his shoulder. He could feel the heat radiating off her forehead, feel the tickle of her hair against his skin.

He had to at least make an attempt. "Should I ask how Harlow is? Or is that off-limits?"

"You really want to know? I thought you hated him. I thought you didn't even think he was real."

"I'm over it."

"Really?"

"Yeah. I've missed you too much to stay angry about anything."

And yes, maybe he was twisting the truth a bit, but he was being entirely honest about his emotions. That's what really mattered. Protecting the connection between the two of them.

"So how's it going with him?"

"I wish I knew," she said.

"You broke up?"

Elena sat up and looked at Jake. He felt a cool emptiness rush in to replace the warmth of her skin on his arm.

"I wouldn't say exactly that we broke up, but . . . he's got a wild streak. He's gotten himself into some sort of . . . situation. I haven't seen him since . . ."

She stopped herself from revealing more, but what she had said was enough for Jake to spin the calculations in his head and note one more convenient alignment between Harlow's and Nathaniel's actions.

"You know what," he said, letting her off the hook. "Let's talk about something else. We should go to Comic-Con this year. Don't you think? I mean, you've wanted to go forever and why not now? We can get Cameron to buy us plane tickets and . . ." He knew he was babbling, but he just kept on going, filling up the space between them with words. "Who would you go as? I think we should be elves, like from *The Lord of the Rings*. But not the obvious ones, not Legolas or whoever. Some elves that only appear on, like, one page in the appendices. Some elves that nobody would recognize. And then we can wander around acting totally shocked when people come up to us not knowing who we're supposed to be."

Elena tilted her head and gazed at him with what he could only understand to be adoration. He wondered if she'd ever let Harlow—or Nathaniel—see this marvelous and unguarded expression on her face. No way. That look was just for him.

"What?" he said, grinning.

"Where've you been all my life?" she said.

"Right here. Always. Right here."

She looped her arm around his and laid her head against his arm again.

They'd reached the old familiar place in their conversation where they knew where each other was without having to speak. Instead, they watched as the sky transformed from golden into a streaky orange and red and purple.

Jake wished they could stay here forever like this. Nestled close, arm in arm. It felt good—not good like pleasurable, more like there was a goodness that existed when they were together that couldn't be re-created any other way. When would she realize this? he wondered. Or was he asking for too much? Maybe he should be thankful for what they had and not worry about pushing it toward something more.

Slowly, almost imperceptibly, Elena flicked her finger across the hair on his arm. Jake wondered if she realized how intimate the gesture was. A few moments later, she allowed herself to wrap her hand around his arm and hold him tighter, massaging his skin. Just like she would if he were her boyfriend, but it was also possible that she was oblivious to the erotic way he was experiencing her touch.

He wondered what she would do if he allowed himself to shift his hand from where it sat on his knee to her smooth tan thigh like he desperately wanted to.

He didn't dare.

He didn't dare move a muscle, didn't dare do any single thing that might bring this exquisite moment to an end.

35

Elena felt the breeze on her face.

As she pedaled her fixed-gear bike past the shadows of the stilt houses of the Slats, making her way toward the slope that would take her home, she felt a kind of calm she hadn't experienced in weeks.

It was funny. She'd missed the stability she felt in knowing Jake was always there. What she hadn't realized was that she missed all these other things about him. The way he moved his long, knobby arms around, not knowing where to put them. His sad, soulful face and the way, when he became inspired—like he did today talking about Comic-Con—it would betray with a mischievousness so subtle that nobody but her could see.

She imagined him with elf ears on his big round head and laughed out loud at the image.

Most of all, she'd missed his caution—the careful way he absorbed the details of her life and made observations she knew she could trust. Just talking to Jake calmed her down, even if nothing got resolved. He hadn't given her any specific advice—he hadn't needed to—but she knew now that she was strong and sharp enough to persuade her father to give Nina another chance. She'd slather on the charm. If need be, she'd put herself on the line and tell him that he could blame her for whatever trouble Nina caused this time.

Turning up Sunrise Avenue, which cut diagonally across town on a slow rise until it eventually looped around Seminole Park and was the quickest way to get to Greenvale Street, she leaned into her handlebars and let herself grin like a delirious fool.

The whole thing had felt so warm and safe. So intimate. So natural. Was this what Nina had meant when she'd told Elena that Jake was in love with her? That he'd accept whatever craziness was going on in her life without any judgment? Well, there was also the way he looked at her. She'd noticed today that his eyes lingered slightly longer than they had to on her bare thighs, that he had surreptitiously sized up her breasts. He'd desired her, no question. And she had to admit that she liked the feeling of being looked at by him. She liked the thought that he might go home and replay his time with her today, that he might ache for her and wish he could touch her and kiss her like he wanted to. She liked the power of knowing that he wouldn't dare, that he was powerless to do anything with his love for her. It was all very erotic in a kind of cruel psychosexual way, and she felt a little bit wrong just noticing it. She didn't want to ever become the kind of person who would take advantage of Jake's desire.

As she made her way up the hill, her legs burned a little more with each turn of the pedals. She crossed A Street Southwest against the light. She was out of the Slats now, in the no-man's-land between the two neighborhoods where the blocks went on forever and the boxy beige buildings of Maritime Industrial Park sprawled like tombstones. Halfway home.

She wondered if Jake had noticed her finger on his arm. She hadn't meant anything sexual by it. She'd just felt close to him. But thinking about it now, she couldn't deny that it had been sort of sexy. Had she been teasing him? She hadn't meant to tease him.

Her phone vibrated in the front pocket of her jean shorts.

Slipping off the pedals, she let the bike roll to a stop and planted one foot on the pavement, straddling the bike while she pulled the phone out to see who was calling. Jake? Nina?

No. It was Harlow.

A flare went off in her head, sending her reeling, erasing all thoughts of Jake.

"Jesus," she said, when she answered. "I thought you'd died." She was only half joking.

"No," he said. "Not yet. How's tricks? I've missed you."

He was trying to play it off like his disappearing act was a normal thing to do. No way was she going to let him off the hook this easily.

"What the hell, Harlow?" she said. "You turn into a pumpkin at the stroke of midnight and the only explanation I get is 'I've missed you'?"

He didn't respond at first. She could hear him struggling with how to go about explaining himself. "I wanted to call earlier, but . . . it wasn't safe."

"You could at least tell me what's going on . . . Harlow?" Had she lost him again?

"Yeah. I'm here," he said, finally. He was whispering now. "I'm trying to figure how where to start. I guess, with that guy I saw at the hotel on New Year's Eve. It's crazy. *He's* crazy. He's all hooked in with the Cuban mob. He thinks I owe him a hundred thousand dollars."

"Oh shit." Elena's heart raced. "What did you do? How did that happen?"

"Nothing! I don't know!" Harlow whispered emphatically. "I met him in a club in Miami one night and he seemed like a good guy. We had a couple of drinks and talked about baseball and suddenly he was accusing me of being involved with some other gang he was at war with. He went totally insane. Started waving a gun around. And he's been after me ever since. Somehow he got my number. And my address. A guy like that, he really would kill me. That's why I haven't been in touch. I had to leave town. And I can't come home unless I give him the money or . . . I don't know."

Her brain couldn't process what he was telling her fast enough. The whole thing sounded far-fetched until she remembered the stories her father used to tell her about how ruthless the mob had been when he was growing up in Miami, how he'd had to watch his back every second of the day and be prepared to fight over the smallest, most inconsequential insult.

"God, that's horrible," said Elena. "You should have called me. I've been worried. I mean, I thought we . . ." She stopped herself from saying anything embarrassing about relationships and her own hurt expectations. Instead she said, "I'm on your side, remember? And didn't you tell me I was the only one you could trust?"

"Yeah. Sorry. I've got issues. Listen—"

She wasn't done chastising him. Suddenly she understood how Nina felt with Matty. She just had to get it out of her system. "If you trust me, you shouldn't disappear like that. Or anyway, you should take me with you."

"You're right. It's just, it's dangerous. I'd hate for anything to happen to you."

"Where are you? I want to see you."

"That's not a good idea right now. I mean, it's impossible. Listen, I've only got a couple minutes to talk." She could hear an urgent, anxious edge in his voice now. "I need to know if I can really trust you."

"I just told you you could."

"Even if things get real? 'Cause shit's starting to get pretty real right now."

"You can trust me, Harlow. I promise."

She stood there, still straddling her bike, in the growing darkness, waiting. She was suddenly aware of how empty the street was. How dark. There were streetlamps every fifty yards or so, but anything could be lurking in the darkness between them. She hopped off the bike and began walking it up the hill, eager to get herself locked up safely at home as quickly as possible.

When he finally spoke again, he said, "I knew I could. It's just hard to believe. You're . . . you're the only one. I'm not used to it." He paused and she could hear his head spinning in the silence. "Thank you," he said.

"So tell me what I can do. Let me help you."

"Okay," he said. "I've been scrambling to find some way to at least buy myself some time."

"And?"

"And I've figured out who he's sent to hurt me. One

of them goes to Chris Columbus, actually. I think there might be a way to scare him off. If you're willing to do one tiny thing for me."

"Sure," Elena said, gulping. "Anything."

"Okay. I don't know the guy's name, but I know he drives a black Mini with a checkerboard hood . . ."

36

The Roderick School's campus sprawled across fifty acres of wooded hills on the outskirts of Atlanta. Its brick colonial buildings, which reminded the students of the long tradition they were a part of and, theoretically, inspired a sense of pride and respect in them, were clustered around one corner of the estate. The rest of the land was there for strolling, daydreaming, pickup games of soccer and lacrosse, and, if you were Nathaniel, who knew every inch of the place, hiding out among the oaks and smoking cigarettes.

His favorite spot for this was a shady patch of dirt encircled by trees out past the track field. He and his friends had been coming here since freshman year.

They'd carted logs in to use as makeshift chairs. They'd found a squirrel hole in one of the gnarled old oaks in which to hide their cigarettes and their stashes of drugs.

And just because Nathaniel had been caught flouting the rules once—well, he'd been caught many more times than once, but he'd been suspended once—didn't mean he had any intention of giving up his vices.

As he explained to his friend and sometimes client in the Adderall trade, Alex, a stocky guy with dark preppy hair and permanently blushing cheeks, "What's the point of living if you aren't having fun while you do it?"

It the last day before the new semester would start, and they'd snuck out here to avoid the tedium of Sunday-morning chapel. They were sitting next to each other on one of the logs and as he spoke, Nathaniel poked idly at the dirt with a stick he'd picked up somewhere.

"I don't know, man," Alex said. He had a weird way of holding his cigarette like a joint when he smoked, which made him look like a con man, always afraid the cops were around the corner. "I'd be worried that now that you've been kicked out once, they'll do something even worse next time they catch you."

"Like what? Call the cops? They can't call the cops. They're too afraid of the bad publicity that would create. Anyway, Cameron gave them enough money to build a new campus on Mars if they wanted."

"What about college? They could screw you there."

"Not likely," Nathaniel said, laughing scornfully. "I'm a Stanford legacy. There's a dorm there named after Cameron." He pulled his flask out of the back pocket of his jeans and took a long pull. "Want some? It's Grey Goose."

"It's ten in the morning," said Alex skeptically.

Nathaniel shrugged and threw back another slug of vodka. He drew a face in the dirt and added shaggy hair to it so it would look vaguely like Jake.

Alex shook his head in wonder. "Must be nice," he said. "I'd lose my scholarship in a second if I got caught doing half the shit you get away with."

"Yeah, well, you know," Nathaniel said. He lit another cigarette and took a long satisfying drag. "It's not all fun and games. Cameron's planning to torpedo my trust fund."

"You're kidding."

"Totally not kidding. His new wife's got this son who's, like . . . I guess Cameron pities the guy or something. Kid can do no wrong."

"Dude," said Alex. "What are you going to do?"

Nathaniel idly jabbed the sharp end of his stick at the face he'd drawn in the dirt, poking its eyes out, slashing at its mouth. Then he smiled a malevolent smile.

"I've already done it. Bro's in love with some chicky. A totally naïve, anime geek girl. I fucked her last week. Or let me rephrase that. A friend of mine, 'Harlow'"—he

made air quotes with his fingers as he said the name—
"fucked her. I catfished her. Man, you should have seen
her. I'm telling you, it felt so good to take her away from
him. The power of the penis, brother. She was putty in
my hands."

Alex chuckled cynically. "And?" he said.

"And Harlow's a real bad dude and since she's a naïve
little geeky chicky, she's fallen totally in love with him.
He's in serious trouble and she'll do anything to help
him. She's going to annihilate the threat for me."

"How?"

Nathaniel locked eyes with Alex.

"If I told you that I'd have to kill you." For a second
he held a dead-serious poker face, but then his expression cracked and the self-satisfied smirk that Jake had
come to loathe so much spread across his face. "Let's just
say he's allergic to bees."

37

As Jake drove his shiny new black Mini to school on Monday morning, he marveled again at the Mini's responsiveness. It seemed to know what he was going to do before he did. Tapping the brake at every stoplight, turning the wheel at every corner, he remembered how much effort the same action would have taken with the Rumbler.

He felt guilty liking the car so much, like he was betraying his father somehow, though he knew that was silly. When he'd mentioned his reservations about the Mini to his dad on the phone last night, the old man had laughed and said, "Jake, that old Jeep was a piece of shit two years ago when I gave it to you. By now you must have to stick your feet through the rust holes beneath the driver's seat and drive it *Flintstones* style. It's sweet that you're so worried about my feelings, but take the gift. I would."

It was like Jake had been released. Now that he had his dad's permission to like the Mini, all his sentimentality and weird fears that the Rumbler would feel bad if he abandoned it disappeared just like that.

Jake wasn't the kind of guy who generally drove around town with the stereo turned up so loud that the car shook with sound, but as he navigated the twists and turns of Shore Drive, with the beach on one side and the boutiques on the other, he couldn't help testing what his speakers could do. It was such a novelty—listening to his own music, streaming from his own phone via Bluetooth. Yes, he was listening to the Monsters of Folk rather than the salsa, or hip-hop, or classic rock that usually blared from decked-out speakers, but it still felt good to sing along and tap the beat on the slippery molded steering wheel.

He turned up Pelican and rolled along past the evenly spaced palm trees in the median.

He kept noticing more aspects of the experience.

For example, the soft leather driver's seat was so cozy. He'd worried that, given how the Mini was so small and he was so tall, he'd have to fold himself like a fan to fit inside, but it turned out there was a lot more space than there appeared to be.

Or the old-school feel of the small, boxy mirrors.

And that smell. There was nothing quite like that new-car smell.

When his phone dinged with a new text message, the sound carried through the car stereo, such an upgrade over the old tape deck system of the Rumbler. He wondered if it was Elena, checking in like she used to do in the morning, wondered if they'd left the discord of Christmas break far enough behind to resume their old rituals.

Jake was a conscientious driver. Much as he might want to, he resisted checking to see who the text was from. There'd be time for that later, when he got to school. Right now he was too busy savoring how cool he felt driving a Mini Cooper around town, heading to school from the north, where the rich kids lived, rather than from the southwest, where people like him came from.

He could see Chris Columbus up ahead, the faded tan and blue buildings lined up like shoe boxes. The quads crawling with students searching for their friends. The hill and the glimmering theater complex sitting atop it like some sort of temple.

He turned onto the unnamed access road that

separated the parking lot from the school's campus, slowing to make way for the students traipsing across it. He peered through the throngs, hoping to see Elena somewhere, but all he saw were people he didn't know. As he waited for an opening in which he could turn into the lot, he couldn't help imagining them gawking at him sitting in his Mini. He felt conspicuous, notable, important in some new mysterious way.

He crawled through the parking lot looking for a space and finally found one way near the back in the northeast corner. And turning off the engine, he finally checked his text messages.

Sadly, no word from Elena, but second best, it was Arnold. Finally.

Jake did a quick survey of the Mini to see if it had accumulated any dirt in the fifteen minutes it had been on the road. A new car was like a new pair of sneakers—you dread the moment that it gets its first scratch. It looked good, though. Still pristine for now.

Then, hoofing it through the lot, Jake tapped through to see what Arnold had to say.

"I HAVE THE DROIDS YOU'VE BEEN LOOKING FOR."

Oh, Arnold, Jake thought, *if only we could all be as awkward as you.* He'd thought a lot about the plan he'd hatched with Arnold in the two days since he and Elena had met at the pier. Part of him had felt he should call Arnold off. Now that he and Elena had made up, he didn't want to do anything that might push her away again. But if his suspicions were true and Harlow was really Nathaniel—God. He had to find out for his own sake as much as Elena's.

He wrote Arnold back. "GREAT! MEET FOR LUNCH?"

"YES," Arnold responded. Then he added, "YOU WILL BE PLEASED."

Jake smiled. It took everything in his power to resist texting Elena right that second to tell her the bad-good news. But no. That would be jumping the gun. And it would upset her. He didn't want her to think he was back to obsessively prodding her about Harlow.

He put his phone away. He felt unstoppable. Like he was, at least momentarily, king of the world.

All morning, Elena had tingled with anticipation, feeling weirdly jittery, as though she were the one in extreme danger.

She'd been extra-conscious of the larger, tougher Cuban dudes wandering around campus, sizing up each one and wondering if he might be the guy Harlow was worried about. It could be anyone. Maybe some little weasely guy like Matty. And the most unnerving thing was that everyone looked so normal. Nobody was wearing a sign above his head saying, *This one, he's a foot soldier for the Cuban mob.* And yet, every guy she walked past felt like a threat.

To calm her nerves, she tried to put a positive spin on

her fear. It might be a good omen. It meant that maybe nobody could tell what she was planning, either.

When the time came for her to cross the quad toward the parking lot during second period—her free period—Elena reminded herself to look normal.

Be casual, she told herself. *Don't do anything to draw attention to yourself. All that spy stuff, that ducking and weaving and hiding behind bushes, will just make people wonder what you're doing. Act like you've forgotten something in your car. Don't be self-conscious. Walk tall. Take your time.*

She couldn't help thinking that everyone was watching her, though. She had to hold her messenger bag in front of her, hugging it tight so that the jar in which she'd captured the ten bees wouldn't jostle too much. Talk about conspicuous.

Paying special attention to the balls of her feet, the way they hit the ground and rolled with each step she took, she regulated her gait and carved an even, straight path through the grass of the quad and across the road into the parking lot. As far as she could tell, nobody had noticed her so far, but knowing this did nothing to lessen her creeping paranoia.

There must have been four hundred cars in the lot. Standing on her tiptoes, Elena tried to survey the field, but she wasn't anywhere near tall enough to see over the

SUVs. She'd have to walk the aisles and hope that she got lucky.

She turned down one aisle, then another, and another and another and another, noting and crossing each car off.

No one was around but her, thank God, but time seemed to be moving very slowly, like each ticking second might expose her.

Another aisle and another. She began to wonder if the guy had skipped school today.

Then, finally, she saw it. A black Mini Cooper tucked away in the far northeast corner of the lot.

Her heart felt like it was trying to punch its way out of her chest. She sped her pace. She couldn't help it.

When she reached the Mini, she crouched next to the passenger-side door so that she was out of sight from the school. She flipped open the flap of her messenger bag. She put on the cracked old work gloves she'd stolen from her dad's toolbox.

Trying the door, she found that it was unlocked. Good old Chris Columbus. No one ever locked their doors.

Very carefully, she lifted the jar of bees out of the bag and placed it on the passenger's seat. Then, rooting around, she found the piece of cardboard she'd brought with her.

Tipping the jar lid down, she watched the bees react to having been jostled. They rose toward the top, like she'd thought they would. They flew repeatedly into the glass, bumping their heads against it like they thought they could break free. She unscrewed the lid and tilted it open slightly, just wide enough to slip the cardboard in, and then she edged the lid away until the only thing keeping the bees captive was her hand clamping the cardboard to the opening.

Then she set the jar open side down on the floor in front of the passenger-side seat and slid the cardboard away.

She shut the door gently and race-walked quickly back toward school.

By the time she got back to the quad, the tension that had been humming through her body was replaced by a rush of self-loathing.

What would happen next unfurled in front of her like a sick film. When the guy who owned the car drove it away, he'd take a hard turn and topple the jar. The bees would escape. They'd be angry. They'd buzz around the car. Even if the guy realized what was going on, even if he immediately rolled down the window, there was no way he'd be able to get them all out. They'd sting him. At least one of them would sting him. And then . . . best not to think about what would happen then.

What if this guy, whoever he was, had a bee allergy?

She'd seen how Jake seized up when a bee hovered near him. He'd told her that one sting might kill him. No matter how much she wanted to help Harlow send these guys a message, she didn't want to kill anyone.

But maybe she already had.

39

"Can we get to the point, please?" Jake said, exasperated. Lunch was almost over and he still didn't know anything.

Finding Arnold had wasted the first ten minutes. He'd taken this spying thing way too literally. He'd chosen the farthest corner table of the cafeteria, a tiny two-seater that was half-hidden behind a massive easel on which a sign had been mounted announcing the winter dance next week. He'd also put on a too-large pair of aviator sunglasses and kept his head ducked, cupping a hand across his forehead in some weird attempt to hide himself further.

Once Jake had sat down, he'd had to listen to Arnold

babble for half an hour, first admitting that he hadn't known how to hack when he'd agreed to help, and then excitedly detailing every tiny nuance and every incremental step involved putting together the information in the manila envelope he still clutched like nuclear secrets under the table.

"I'm not trying to be rude," Jake added, knowing how easy it was to hurt Arnold's feelings. "It's just, we only have so much time. I have to get to chem in ten minutes."

Arnold fingered the envelope and peered at Jake over his aviators. "Is it safe?"

"Arnold! Arnold, why wouldn't it be safe? Nobody knows what we're talking about. And even if they knew, the only person who would care is Elena, and"—Jake craned his head around, making his point—"she's not here!"

"Well . . ."

"Arnold."

"Okay." Arnold slid the envelope toward Jake under the table, poking it at Jake's knee until Jake snatched it away.

As Jake leafed through thick stack of documents stuffed into the envelope, he could feel Arnold's eyes on him, waiting for approval.

It was all there. IP addresses. Locations of servers tracking Harlow's coordinates when he sent this or that message to Elena. Screenshots of Nathaniel's computer. Everything Jake needed to prove to Elena that Harlow was Nathaniel.

For a moment Jake got hung up on a long, revolting email thread between Nathaniel and some guy named Bingham Prescott in which Nathaniel went on and on about Elena, taking a malicious glee in the charge he'd gotten out of stealing her out from under Jake's nose. Some of the things Nathaniel had written were so obscenely cruel that Jake wanted to strangle him. "I'm telling you, bro, she's so short it was like fucking a garden gnome," he said at one point. And "Let me know if you want a taste. She'll do anything for me. I'll pass her off to you."

Jake bit back his rage. "Thanks," he said to Arnold, flushing.

He was surprised that he wasn't happier about having been proved right. He felt vindicated, but in a sour way.

Suddenly panicked, he wondered if maybe he shouldn't tell her at all, if maybe what he should do is find some way to secretly stop Nathaniel without Elena knowing.

No. She deserved to know. But he could just imagine how she would react when he told her the news. She'd be angry at first for his revealing truths she didn't want to accept. And that would be horrible. But what would be even worse would be the moment when she realized that

"Harlow" had only been pretending to care for her, that really he'd been trying to hurt Jake. She'd feel invaded, used.

"Did I do good?" Arnold asked. "You look like you're going to barf."

"No, I'm okay." Jake caught sight of himself in Arnold's aviators. He really did look pale. "Arnold, really," he said, smiling weakly. "This is exactly what I needed."

Arnold grinned. Then he leaned forward and stared at the table for a long minute as though this small praise from Jake was so overwhelming that he'd had to shut his whole system down to deal with it. When he looked up again, he said, "Are you really going to write a song about me now?"

"Sure. Absolutely. It'll be great. I promise. But listen, it still needs an ending, don't you think? I mean, you've uncovered the bad guy, but if we want the song to have a happy ending, there should be some way to get back at him, don't you think?"

Arnold flashed his evil-genius expression. He maniacally drummed the tips of his fingers together. "I've been thinking about that," he said.

40

"I did something really bad," Elena said, whispering into the phone even though she'd tucked herself away behind some bushes in a corner of the back quad where the students at Chris Columbus almost never went. It was her free period and with nothing to do but think, she was beginning to panic about what she'd done that morning.

"Don't say that," Nina said from the other end of the line.

Elena could hear the TV blaring in the background. She felt like she was going to hyperventilate and she tried to control her breathing.

"You don't understand, Nina. I really did."

She squeezed her eyes shut, but this just allowed the horrors that had been burning through her brain to project themselves across her eyelids—visions of bees swarming that little black Mini, of the guy who owned it, whoever it was (she imagined him to be a massive hulk of a man, one of those Cubanos who still dressed for the island in linen chinos and a bleached white tank top), frantically trying to swipe them away and struggling to unlock the door as they dive-bombed toward his face, his car swerving, crashing, a mangle of steel, and him unconscious and bleeding behind the airbag.

It was like it had already happened, like the guy was already dead. No one deserved that. And the thought that she was the one who caused it . . . Elena felt rancid, like there was evil growing in her bones.

Nina sighed dismissively. "There's nothing to worry about," she said. "I'm done with Matty. For real this time. I'm not going to let him set foot in the house."

"I'm not talking about that." Over the weekend, Elena had managed to calm her father down and convince him to let Nina move back in. The deal she'd made was that if Nina messed up again he could blame Elena and as punishment, take her computer away.

"Well, good," said Nina, "because I'm already all packed and ready for you to help me move this afternoon."

Elena heard Nina's words, but it was like her voice

269

was coming from underneath the ocean, like her concerns were so remote that they weren't quite real. "Yeah," she said. "I'll be there after school. Don't worry."

"Okay, good," Nina said. Her tone softened and turned maternal. "What happened?"

Elena's head was swimming with guilt and shame and fear. She was afraid to say what she'd done out loud. It was as though, if she refused to say it, there might be a chance that it hadn't really happened. But she had to say it. She *had* to. "God, I feel like I'm going to throw up. Nina, it's so bad what I did. I feel like I've put some sort of hole in the universe and I'm going to explode as I'm sucked through it."

"What happened?" Nina said again. "Tell me. We'll make it all better."

Elena stood up from her crouch behind the bushes and looked around. It was one of those perfect warm, dry, sunny winter days. How ironic. The few students she could see weren't paying attention to her. Some guys were throwing a Frisbee back and forth. There was a girl reading something on her iPad under a tree, but she was far enough away that she wouldn't be able to hear.

She dove in and blurted it all out, how Harlow had been in trouble and she'd wanted to help him, how she'd broken into the Mini, how she'd planted the bees. "Why?!" she sobbed. "Why did I do that? And what kind of person is Harlow to ask the girl he's supposedly in a relationship with to do something like this?"

"Well—" Nina said, but Elena cut her off.

"The worst thing is that while I was sneaking out to the parking lot, I knew I shouldn't be doing it, but I did it, anyway. Like I didn't have a choice. You know what I mean? Like I was betraying everything that makes me *me*. Isn't that horrible?"

"That's what happens when you date a guy like Harlow," Nina said. "I would know. Let me ask you a question."

"Okay."

"I've been thinking about this all week. Since you came over crying on New Year's Eve."

"Yeah?"

"What are you doing with a dude like Harlow? He's not your type at all. He's more my speed, and you know where that gets you."

"I . . . I don't know," Elena said. The knot in her stomach tightened a little. She'd been asking herself the same questions ever since she'd planted the bees.

"Don't you think that's a problem?"

"He's . . . I mean, he's very cool. He's exciting," she said weakly.

"So exciting that you've gone and done something you already regret to try and please him. Anyway, since when have you been interested in cool? Cool is for shallow people who don't know how to want anything else out of life. You've got your life together. You've got a future. The things that come out of your imagination—they're beautiful. I couldn't begin to do something like that. You've got good taste, when you trust it."

"What's that supposed to mean?" Elena asked. She felt defensive, like she had to fight for her relationship with Harlow, but at the same time, she knew already that Nina was right about him and that however she'd felt about him before, her relationship with him was ruined now. She'd never be able to look at him again without seeing the person who'd asked her to put bees in some-body's car.

"What I mean is, it seems like with this Harlow guy, you're trying to be someone you're not."

Just then, Elena's phone vibrated.

"Hold on," she told Nina.

It was a text from Jake. "YOU FREE NEXT PERIOD? I NEED TO TALK TO YOU!"

Typing quickly so she could get back to her conversation with Nina, Elena responded. "I'VE GOT TRIG. I'LL DING YOU LATER."

"Who was that?" her sister asked when she returned to the call.

"Just Jake."

"'Just Jake,'" Nina teased. "What? You asked me what I meant by 'You've got good taste.' Well, there you go."

"Nina, come on," Elena said, realizing what her

sister was implying. A flash of memory, the sensation of laying her head on Jake's arm when they'd been at the pier last weekend, burned through Elena's mind. She remembered how her skin had tingled on the bike ride home. Maybe she *had* felt something more than friendship. But still, she felt she had to defend herself. "Jake's like a brother. He's . . . I've known him since I was a baby. And . . . there's no mystery or surprises with him. He practically . . ." She stopped herself from saying *knows me better than I know myself.* She realized that was a losing argument. She was blushing and she was glad Nina couldn't see her. "Anyway," she went on, "I'm a Rios girl. We don't date nice guys."

"Maybe we should start. I think it's about time for us to be treated the way we deserve to be treated."

Elena didn't know what to say to that. She felt better, but why? It was like she'd suddenly gotten permission to let down her guard and open her heart in a way she'd always secretly wanted to.

"Okay," Elena said in embarrassment. "Can we change the subject?"

The phone still jammed to her ear, she squeezed out from behind the bushes to head toward Mr. Conner's trigonometry classroom. It occurred to her that talking about Jake like this had managed to take her mind off her crime for a moment, but knowing that she was able to forget about it just made her feel guiltier about what she'd done.

Nina chuckled. "Sure," she said. "What do you want to talk about?"

"Oh, I don't know. What I should do about those bees, maybe?"

"Do you think you can get them out of the car?"

"It would be hard. I just spent my last free period talking to you. Now I've got to go to class."

"Well, you know, I think you're blowing this up into something bigger than it is. It's more of a prank than a real threat to the guy. He's probably going to see the jar. Even if he doesn't, the odds of him being allergic are very, very low. Bees get stuck in cars all the time without everybody in the car dying."

"Jake's allergic," Elena said.

"Well, it's not Jake's car, is it? I mean, you would have noticed if you were putting bees in the Rumbler."

"That's true. And as far as I know, Jake's not in the Cuban mob."

"Don't worry about it. Elena? Really. Let's call it a learning experience."

A learning experience. Elena liked that idea, even if she wasn't sure she could bring herself to be as cavalier as Nina was urging her to be.

"I can try," she said.

41

Jake didn't hear back from Elena until sixth period, when his phone buzzed loudly enough to provoke a sharp, disapproving look from Mr. Lester.

"NOW A GOOD TIME? LOTS TO TALK TO YOU ABOUT, TOO!"

Maneuvering the phone into the hollow metal tray under the desk, Jake tried to be as inconspicuous as he could while he picked out his response.

"STUCK IN CALCULUS," he said. "AFTER SCHOOL?"

He glanced toward the front of the room, where Mr. Lester was writing an equation on the board with his back turned. He was known around campus as being cranky but absentminded, and Jake was glad this was turning out to be true. Still, he held the phone in his hand under the desk so that it wouldn't clatter again when Elena's response came in.

"HAVE TO RUN AFTER SCHOOL. HELPING NINA MOVE BACK HOME."

Jake typed quickly. "YOU HAVE YOUR DAD'S CAR?"

"YEAH."

"WALK YOU TO THE PARKING LOT?"

"SURE! MEET YOU IN THE QUAD."

"Are you done, Mr. Gordon?"

Lester was glaring at him, arms crossed, a grimace pulling his walrus mustache down to his chin. Jake could feel everyone in the classroom turning to look at him. He heard snickers from the back of the room.

"Yeah," Jake said, turning beet red. "I'm done." Then, for good measure, he added, "Sorry."

He slipped his phone into the pocket of his jeans and sat up straighter in his seat, trying to look like he was paying serious attention.

He wasn't, of course. He was tangled in his thoughts. Now that he and Elena had made a date, he had to make up his mind about whether or not to go through with telling her what he'd learned about Harlow. He'd flip-flopped five times already today, and he could feel his mind changing again now. He had to tell her. It would be dishonest, unfair, patronizing of him not to.

Jake. Jake Gordon.

The name floated through Elena's head again as she was jostled in the mob trying all at the same time to push their way through the doorway out of Ms. Samson's AP English classroom.

The warm, happy bubble floated up her chest again and she allowed herself a small private smile.

Good ol' Jake.

She squeezed past Dev Mehta and his oversized headphones out onto the covered walkway in front of the classroom. She hiked her backpack up on her shoulder and headed, with a little bop in her step, across the lawn, toward the front quad, where she'd told Jake she'd meet him.

It was all so weird but at the same time so obvious and right. Since talking to Nina that morning, she'd felt like she'd been liberated, like she'd been walking around all this with a plastic bag tied around her head and now it had been ripped off and she could finally breathe. How had Nina known? And more important, how had Elena *not* known?

Pausing to look up at the cloudless sky, she felt the gushing emotion crash over her again.

And there it was again. *Jake.*

She'd depended on him for such a long time. Even when she was alone he was there with her, draping his arm over her shoulder, whispering his quiet opinions in her ear, coloring her way of looking at absolutely everything that happened in her life. If she was being honest with herself—and now, finally, she was—she couldn't imagine being in the world without Jake by her side. Was that love? Was that friendship? Throughout the day she'd begun to think that maybe there was no difference between the two.

Picking up her pace, she turned the corner around the cafeteria and arrived at the edge of the quad. It was flooded with people, every student at Chris Columbus, six hundred students, all pushing as one toward the parking lot where the buses were lined up on one side and the cars were parked tight around them.

Standing on her tiptoes, hopping to see above the throngs of students, she searched for Jake.

He wasn't hard to find. Standing a foot taller than everyone around him, he rose like an island out of the flowing sea. Students parted around him and reconvened on the other side. He was wearing his sunglasses, his hair flopping down over his left eye in that way that it did. And he had that expression on his face, that look of slightly mystified innocence that he always fell into in his most unguarded moments. She knew this look so well. It just hadn't made her swoon like this before now.

And the feeling totally surprised her.

Gulping down a deep breath, trying to control the joy leaping through her bloodstream, Elena practically dove into the crowd, weaving and dodging toward him.

Every few feet she paused to check his location. In a typically Jake-like way, he was holding tight. Surveying the faces in this or that direction. That was just like him, wasn't it? Sturdy, careful, and full of faith that if he held to what he knew was right, everything would work out. Here came that trill in her chest again. It wasn't the urgent chaos she'd thought love was supposed to create, more a tickle of recognition, like, *There he is. I'm safe now. I know who I am again.*

She zigzagged around so that she could come up on Jake from behind. Ducking around a group of fifteen cheerleaders all decked out in variations on the same ruffled skirt, she snuck up to his right and tapped him playfully on the left shoulder. When he turned to see who was there, she tapped his right shoulder and ducked to the left. He turned again, and she dipped her head cutely into her shoulders, stuck her tongue out, and made a funny face.

"Gotcha," she said. She knew she was grinning like a fool, but she didn't care.

"Wow, you're in a good mood," Jake said. "Did something happen?"

"I . . . Yeah," she said. "Let me look at you first."

Elena stepped back so she could study him. She wanted to memorize this moment. The earnest, slightly quizzical expression on his face as he waited to hear what she had to tell him, the soft kindness around his eyes, the light brown hair, just a touch too long, flopping down over his round forehead. His face wasn't traditionally handsome—it was better than that: interesting, magnetic. It had character. She could stare at it forever without ever getting bored.

"What?" Jake said. "Do I have ketchup on my chin? I do, don't I? Shit."

As he rubbed at his chin trying to rid himself of the phantom ketchup, she bit her lip to keep herself from laughing.

"Where is it? Did I get it off?"

Elena tipped her head and grinned at him. "There's

no ketchup on your face, Jake."

"What is it, then? You're being weird. You're staring at me funny."

"I've been thinking about the other day," she said. "At the pier. I've been thinking there's something I should have done."

"Oh? What's that?"

"Just . . . this."

Leaping, she spread her arms and hoped he'd catch her. When he did, she wrapped her legs around his waist.

She looked him straight in the eye and held his surprised gaze for a second. Then, just as he was about to say something, she kissed him like she'd never kissed anyone before, pouring all of the emotions that had building up throughout the day into him through her lips.

It took him a second to catch up to what was going on, but he held her tight and kissed her back with a timid tenderness.

She slipped down his hips. As he hiked her back up, he lost his balance and they hobbled, almost tumbling into the grass, but they didn't stop kissing. They explored each other's lips with their own until Elena slipped down and stood on her own two feet.

"I should invest in a ladder," Elena said. She reached up and ran her palm along the stubble on Jake's cheek.

And then, almost exactly at the same time, they began to giggle.

"Is this really happening?" Jake whispered, bending down to rest his chin against Elena's forehead.

"Does it feel like it's happening?"

"Yes."

"I guess it must really be happening, then," said Elena. "Sorry it took me so long," she added. "I've been an idiot."

Sympathy and concern and something like acceptance floated through Jake's eyes. Then he smiled softly and kissed her again.

They stood there, Jake hunched over to meet Elena on her level, her perched on her tiptoes, bracing herself on his shoulders, and gazed at each other, barely conscious of the students stepping around them.

"What did you have to talk to me about?" she asked.

"Nothing." He paused, thinking for a moment, struggling with himself. "It doesn't matter now."

She didn't push him further. She suspected it must have something to do with his fixation on Harlow, and he was right, it didn't matter now.

Reluctantly, she pulled away from him but she couldn't bring herself to let go of his hand. "I should go," she said. "I have to go help Nina."

"You want a ride?"

"No. Dad lent me the Volvo, remember? Anyway, I should do it alone. She needs me right now."

"Okay, then." He pulled her to himself and squeezed her tight again. "I can at least walk you to the parking lot, yeah?"

"Yeah."

Entering the stream of students, they made their way slowly down the hill toward the parking lot. Halfway there, Jake shyly pressed his index finger into Elena's palm. She squeezed it briefly, and then laced her hand around his.

And there was that trill in her chest again. It wouldn't go away, not even now that they were together.

They crossed the street to the lip of the lot.

"Where you parked?" he asked.

"Over there." She pointed to an area behind the buses. "You?"

Waving vaguely toward the northeast corner, he said, "Thattaway."

He released her hand.

"I guess this is it, then," he said.

She made a face, teasing him lightly for his lack of confidence. "That's it, Jake? No. This is just the beginning," she said. "Unless you decide to run back to that girlfriend in the Keys." She winked.

He blushed and dipped his head in embarrassment. "Yeah, well . . . ," he mumbled.

"Hey," she said softly. She touched her fingertips to

his chin and guided his face until she could look into his eyes again.

They kissed one last long time and she felt herself swoon. "I'll call you later," she said, reluctantly pulling away from him.

"Okay," he said. "Good luck with Nina."

And that was it. He squeezed her shoulder and they separated, walking in their different directions toward their cars, picking their way through the traffic jam that had developed in the lot.

Elena couldn't help pausing after a few steps to glance back at him and take one more look. She was pleased to see that he'd done the same thing. They grinned. They waved at each other.

Okay, she told herself. *Enough.*

Padding across the gravel toward her dad's car, she willed herself not to look back again. She had her whole life to gaze at him.

The events of that morning seemed very far away now—Harlow and his desperate situation and the actions she'd taken to help him that morning, they all seemed like a bad dream that she'd thankfully woken up from. Nina was right. The whole thing had been a childish prank, something that she shouldn't have done, but what was the worst that could happen? A bad person would be stung by a couple of bees. It wasn't like she'd killed anybody. All that was left to do was to tell Harlow it was over.

Still, she couldn't help but wonder who owned that Mini and if he'd ever find out that she was the one who'd sabotaged his car. She turned one more time and peered toward the back corner of the lot, where she knew the Mini was parked.

In a blissful daze, Jake squeezed around the cars jammed at every angle trying to get the quickest jump on the exit from the parking lot. He couldn't help thinking that somewhere along the line, right around when Elena had kissed him, reality had split in two and he'd floated away from the world as it existed, into some other region where everything was impossibly perfect and beautiful. He felt like he was riding through a dream.

When he reached the car—another fantastically great thing that had suddenly appeared to change his life—he studied its gleaming checkerboard hood and let himself feel the amazing sensations flowing through his body. He could only describe them as Wow. The physical incarnation of Wow.

He settled into the driver's seat and turned the car on. He wasn't seeing anything except the visions in his head of himself and Elena riding off into the future. It was too good to be true. Everything about his life right this moment was way, way, way, way too good to be true.

He put the car in reverse and, still getting used to the particular touchiness of the Mini's pedals, tapped the gas, sending the car jerking backward with a gravel-churning spin of the tires.

Something toppled on the passenger-side floor. That was odd. He hadn't put anything there. Glancing over, he saw a Mason jar rolling on its side against the well of the door, and then he heard the buzzing inside the car. Where had that come from?

Bees. His heart stopped just for a second.

He tried to roll the windows down, but he still hadn't gotten used to the layout of the buttons, and in his panicked jabbing, he kept locking and unlocking the doors.

They were buzzing around his ears. Pounding their faces repeatedly into the windshield. There seemed to be hundreds of them.

Someone behind him honked his horn.

Jake swatted at the bees, but they just kept coming.

Looking around himself in a panic, he saw the cars

up ahead, inching toward the exit. He saw the students still walking toward their own cars.

He felt a sting on his cheek. Then another one on his elbow.

He could feel his face beginning to swell. As the venom sank in, it felt like someone was pulling barbed wire through his muscles.

He looked around frantically. The students on the other side of the glass, chatting with their friends and walking to their cars, seemed so calm and far away from him. Didn't anybody see what was happening? Wasn't anyone going to help him?

Then he saw Elena. Her dark golden skin. Her short curls. Her big, beautiful black eyes. Maybe he was dreaming.

Wait. She was signaling to him. Was that possible? She was waving her hands out in front of her, racing toward him.

She was crying. She was calling out but he couldn't hear her. He couldn't hear anything. He could barely see her.

Everything was growing blurry. He couldn't see at all.

And then he couldn't breathe, either.

Jake's body was laid out on the hospital bed like a corpse. His face had blown up to twice its usual size. It was red and spongy and his eyes had puffed shut— they bulged like someone had shoved softballs under his skin. The doctors had connected him to what seemed to Elena like a scary number of tubes and sensors.

She had been sitting in the institutional blue chair by his side for the past two hours, staring at him through her tears.

Except for his shallow, rhythmic breathing, he hadn't moved once since they'd let her into the room, and just the sight of him filled Elena with horror over what she'd done. She understood, intellectually, that he was in a coma, but the small percentage chance of him waking up didn't comfort her at all. She couldn't stop thinking about the karmic justice of this happening to him, because of her own stupid actions, as soon as she realized she loved him.

When, eventually, Jake's mother arrived, Elena ran to her before she'd gotten through the door. She squeezed her as tight as it was humanly possible to squeeze and wouldn't let go. She could feel the heaves in Jake's mother's chest as the woman gazed over Elena's head at her immobile son.

"I'm sorry," Elena whispered too quietly for anyone but her to hear.

They stood there, holding each other, Jake's mother patting and smoothing Elena's hair, for a long minute, but no matter how long it was, when she reluctantly let go, it was over too soon.

Stepping back, she made space for Jake's mom to enter the room.

Behind her, a suave, suntanned man wearing a flowing white linen shirt held a massive bouquet of flowers. This must be Cameron. Elena felt a pang of nervousness at finally seeing him in person. This wasn't the context in which she'd wanted to meet him. She wasn't sure how Jake would want her to act around him.

As Jake's mom ran to her son and Cameron busied himself with arranging the flowers on the windowsill,

Elena noticed the shadow of someone else in the hallway, someone lurking there, hidden from view. Whoever it was had almost entered after Cameron and then ducked back out.

Jake's mom took the post Elena had left when she got up to hug her. Cradling Jake's hand between her own, she softly prayed over him.

Cameron pulled a second chair up so he could sit next to her and sympathetically rub her back. "Nathaniel, what's the problem?" he called out to the person in the hallway. "You came all this way, how about you step inside the room and show your respects."

A few seconds later a blond guy with sculpted cheekbones, wearing a black Moschino T-shirt that was more expensive and better tailored than any teenager could possibly need, stepped into the room.

Elena's heart froze. Her whole life froze. Her stomach rolled over itself and she begged herself not to throw up.

It was Harlow.

He turned his head pointedly and looked directly at Elena, saying nothing, showing no recognition, but holding her gaze like he was daring her to expose him. He abruptly cut a jackknife smile and held out his hand to shake. "Nathaniel. Jake's stepbrother."

What could she do? Swallowing back the acid riding up her throat, Elena shook his hand, noting that it was clammy with sweat. "Elena. Jake's *girlfriend*," she said boldly.

She quickly calculated the facts of the situation. Nathaniel was Harlow, which meant Jake had been right all along in his warnings. And if Nathaniel was Harlow, that meant Nathaniel had targeted Jake with the bees, because . . . why? Here she got stuck. He'd wanted to hurt Jake. That was why he'd gone after her and that was why he'd orchestrated this plan with the bees. But what could Jake have done to garner such hatred? She couldn't understand.

She didn't have time to parse through these questions. The doctor had arrived. In his suit and tie and crisp white lab coat, he had a chilly professional air to him.

Jake's mom and Cameron both stood up to talk to him, but he ignored them. He plucked the clipboard on which Jake's chart had been attached and tipped his rectangular glasses onto his forehead to study it, frowning, giving off the sense that he was too busy for small talk.

It was like everyone had entered a state of suspended animation. No one moved. They all just stared at the doctor. Waiting. Waiting. Waiting.

He turned the page. He grimaced.

More waiting.

Elena wanted to scream at him, *Tell us what's happening! Tell us he'll be okay!*

Jake's mom glanced over at her and blinked the tears from her eyes. She reached out and briefly took Elena's hand to calm her.

Finally, the doctor let the clipboard clang back into the plastic slot at the foot of Jake's bed.

He reached a hand out toward Cameron to shake, but Cameron shook his head and, gesturing toward Jake's mom, said, "You should speak to her."

Refocusing, the doctor nodded and said, "Dr. Lawrence." Elena noticed in annoyance that he didn't bother to shake Jake's mom's hand. "Your son's had a severe allergic reaction to four beestings." He went on to list Jake's symptoms, using the polysyllabic technical terms to describe them.

Elena couldn't understand a word he was saying. The longer he went on, the more upset she became. Finally, she couldn't hold it in any longer. "What's that mean, though?" she said, spurting the words out. "Speak English!"

He furrowed his brow and glared at her for a second, then said, "Your friend's brain is in shock. His blood vessels are swelling up. That causes problems with the oxygen flow to his brain and his ability to breathe."

"And?" Jake's mom said.

"And that's it. That's his condition. He's in a coma. We'll see if and when he wakes up."

Before anyone could ask any more questions, he

nodded and strode out of the room the same way he'd entered it.

Elena glanced at Jake's mom. Cameron had her hand sandwiched between his palms and the way he was tending to her made Elena think that he must truly be in love with her. Jake would have liked to know this, she thought. She'd have to tell him when he woke up.

If he woke up. The fact that he might not do this slowly sank into her brain.

It was all too horrible. She squeezed her eyes shut tight and let the emotions roll over her. She gulped down the tears she felt tugging at her throat. It was like trying to hold back the ocean. Letting herself go, she began to sob. And sob. And sob. It was the closest she'd felt to comfort since she'd separated from Jake in the parking lot.

"You okay?" Nathaniel asked. He was leaning casually against the wall like a model posing for a billboard.

Elena shook herself back to the reality of the present situation in the room. "As okay as I can be," she said. She shot Nathaniel a coded look of warning. "Given the fact that my boyfriend's in a coma."

"I know the feeling," Nathaniel said, running his hand through his slicked wavy hair. "I'm pretty torn up myself."

Was he mocking her? His tone could have gone either way. The gall of the guy.

Elena felt a turbulent wave of something new rising

up in her, a revolt in her gut, heat rising in her throat, a clammy suffocating sensation pressing in on her.

She pushed toward the door. Jake's mom, Cameron, even Nathaniel, reached out in concern, asking what was wrong, but she couldn't say. She couldn't speak. She knew if she tried the vomit would rise up and spew all over the linoleum floor.

She shook her head violently and speed-walked out of the room.

Later, as she cradled her head on the toilet seat in the ladies' bathroom and spit the last of her lunch into the bowl, she just felt sicker.

She'd been so stupid. So gullible.

And Nathaniel. He thought Jake's life was just a toy he could play with until he got bored and then he could break it. He didn't even care.

She wondered how she could possibly have been sucked in by him. They'd chatted online all those times. She'd thought he was an artist. And she'd refused to listen to Jake's warnings. She'd let him touch her body. She'd let him—

Here it came again. The nausea. Lunging over the bowl, she tried to let it all out but all that came up were dry heaves and stomach acid.

She vowed to get back at Nathaniel somehow.

If she could.

If it wasn't too late.

45

Later, sitting at a wobbly aluminum table under the dim fluorescent lights of the empty hospital cafeteria, Elena poked at a slimy bowl of cubed honeydew with her spoon. She knew she should eat, but she couldn't bring herself to do so. She didn't feel like she deserved to eat. She didn't deserve nourishment. She didn't deserve anything good in her life after what she'd done—accidentally, she reminded herself—to Jake.

The honeydew was disgusting. She couldn't eat it.

She tried the cottage cheese she'd bought, lifted one halfhearted spoonful to her mouth and moved the watery pebbles around with her tongue. This, at least, she could swallow, but it tasted like sand soaked in sour milk.

Her stomach ached. Her throat felt raw and scratchy. She'd cried herself out and now she just felt like a zombie.

But she had to eat something. She had to stay alive, if for no other reason than to punish Nathaniel and hold vigil over Jake's barely breathing body.

When Elena saw Nathaniel saunter into the cafeteria, wearing his sunglasses like a jackass, she felt the old Rios rage rise up in her. She almost jumped out of her seat to run across the room and claw his eyes out. She couldn't go to war with him. Not here. Not now. The chubby guy at the cash register would see her. She'd be ushered out by security and then everything would be that much worse.

Shaking with repressed anger, she slouched down in her seat and tried to make herself small.

But of course he saw her. The only other person in the room, besides the beleaguered guy working the cash register, was a nervous middle-aged man with a beard who, while pretending to read, had been tapping an incoherent rhythm with his thumb on his tabletop since Elena had arrived.

Nathaniel lifted his sunglasses onto his forehead and pointed at Elena in that way arrogant bros do when they want to look both casual and macho at the same time. He headed right toward her and sat in a splayed-leg stance in the chair across from her.

"What do you want?" Elena hissed, emphatically setting her spoon on the table.

He leaned on his forearms, his hands clasped in front of him, and smirked and stared at her and said not a word.

"If you don't want anything, leave me alone," Elena said.

He just went on smirking.

Elena stared back at him. If this was a staring contest, she refused to lose.

Finally he said, "I guess we're not friends anymore, then."

"Fuck. Off."

"I'll take that as a no. That's fine. I got what I wanted out of you."

Letting her eyes pour acid at him, she refused to dignify that with an answer.

He leaned in closer across the table and studied her like he was looking for a weakness. "You understand, though, that we're not done with each other yet, right?"

"I'm not going to fuck you again," she spit back at him.

Chuckling, he said, "You weren't that good, anyway. I'm talking about the 'accident.'"

298

"Accident. Yeah. Good one." She came close to slapping him, just barely restraining herself.

"See, that's what I mean. We've got unfinished business to discuss."

He disgusted her. She leaned back in her chair to get away from him.

He didn't seem bothered by her revulsion. Adjusting himself in his seat, he pushed forward. "Like I said. We both know it was an accident and that's all anybody else needs to know, too. I need you to promise me that you won't go spreading insidious rumors that this might have been anything else."

"Oh?" she said. "You think you've still got some hold on me? You think you can just snap and I'll do what you say? You don't know me too well, do you?"

Instead of answering, Nathaniel reached down and unlatched the clasp on the black leather messenger bag he'd set on the floor by his feet. He pulled out a large Ziploc bag and placed it on the table. It contained the jar in which Elena had captured the bees.

"I'll tell you what I know," he whispered. "I know that this jar was on the floor of Jake's car. I've got a time stamped photo to prove it."

Elena flinched.

"What? You think I wouldn't have ridden down here to watch? I came back to Dream Point last night. I've spent all day making sure everything went according to the plan. It wasn't hard to sneak up and grab the jar during all the chaos with the paramedics."

He paused and threw Elena a smug smile.

Then, holding the jar up again, he said, "You see that dust clinging to the edges? That's pollen. I'm sure it would be a snap to forensically link it to the dead bees that were also in the car, and that, as you know, were responsible for putting Jake in the hospital. Here's something I'm not sure about, though. Did you wear gloves while you were chasing those bees around your backyard?"

Elena flinched. She gazed at the honeydew. She gazed at the cottage cheese. She thought about throwing them into Nathaniel's face, but she knew that doing so wouldn't accomplish anything. She shuddered a little, and trying not to blink, looked defiantly back up at Nathaniel.

"I didn't think so. See, you're the one who loses if the truth comes out. You did this to him, and you alone."

"Did I?" she asked. "Did I really do it all alone? I'm not so sure about that."

"No? Who'd you conspire with?"

"You!"

He waved his finger critically. "That couldn't be true. I just met you today. You must mean Harlow." He smirked again. "Who doesn't exist."

He had her. She knew it and she knew he knew it, too. The only thing worse than what was happening now would have been for her to break down in tears in front of him. She was glad she'd cried herself out earlier.

"Why did you do this?" she asked him.

Realizing he'd won, Nathaniel allowed himself to slouch back in his chair. "Why not?" he said.

"You've destroyed his life. He's lying there like a vegetable now. The doctor said he might never wake up."

"*I* destroyed his life? I don't think so. That was all you."

"Can you at least stop smirking? I mean, do you have any soul at all?"

He screwed his face up into a softer smile and tipped his head at a sensitive angle. For a moment, Elena saw a trace of the person she'd thought he was when he'd been pretending to be Harlow. Somehow that made everything worse.

"Was any of it true? Anything at all? That story about your friend who died? Or are you just a horrible, evil person who has nothing inside him but hatred and ugliness?"

He patted her hand paternalistically and she recoiled, feeling a spike shoot through her nerves.

When he stood up, the smirk was back. "Thanks for the conversation," he said, packing the jar back into his bag and throwing it over his shoulder. "I think it was exceedingly productive."

With that, he sauntered out like he'd sauntered in, leaving Elena to sit there with her melon and cottage cheese, more alone than she'd ever been in her life.

Nine days later, the only change in Jake's condition was that the swelling had receded. Breathing shallowly, his eyes lightly shut, he looked like himself now, but sadder, lonelier.

Dr. Lawrence, whom Elena still found unnecessarily cold, though she had to admit now that he was excellent at his job, had told her that the internal inflammations had begun to lessen as well. He'd upped the chances of Jake's survival, but warned Elena that he might never wake up from his coma because it was hard to tell how much damage the decreased blood flow to his brain may have caused. So, good and bad news. All they could do now was wait.

Elena held vigil by the side of Jake's bed like she had every day after school since the "accident," giving his mom a break to check in at the café and take care of the life stuff that didn't stop for tragedy. One of the nurses had told her that sometimes music helped stimulate the brain, so today she'd booted up the compilation of songs Jake had given her for Christmas. She'd been listening to them nonstop on her headphones anyway and it seemed right, if poignantly futile, to listen to them together with him, even if he couldn't hear them.

One after the other, Jake's tunes filled the room like ghosts of some present that should have been. "Wake Me When You're Home." "Silly." "Then She Smiled." "I'm Here." "Nothing Doing," with its moody calypso beat. "Saltwater Taffy," the first song he'd ever played for her, sitting in the grass in his backyard on Greenvale Street.

She held his hand, laid her head on his chest, and gazed at his immobile face, letting the music billow around her.

"Misunderstood." "Roll On By." "That's the Way Love Used to Be."

She'd always loved his music, but now it seemed richer, subtler, more beautiful than it ever had before. To think that Sarah in the Keys had really been Elena. That all this was written for her. And that now . . . now it was too late to tell him how much it meant to her.

"Driftwood," the newest one, the one he'd written

while she was stupidly letting herself be drawn in by Harlow, especially broke her heart. She could imagine him sitting alone in that strange impersonal mansion on the shore, staring out at the waves and believing with all his soul that he'd lost her forever.

"Don't let the sea wash me away," he sang.

She kissed his breastbone.

"I won't," she whispered. "I promise. I'll hold you tight. I'll swim you back to shore."

She kissed him again and let the song wash over her.

"Just stay with me," she said. "I need you. I can't survive here without you."

She squeezed his hand and she felt a brief, weak pressure on the soft spot behind her thumb. He hadn't opened his eyes. He hadn't moved in any other way, but still, she wondered, was that him squeezing back? She willed it to be true.

Squeezing again, she sat up and waited for a response.

"Jake?" she said. "Jaybird?"

Nothing.

Then, just as she was about to give up and reconcile herself to the possibility that she'd imagined him communicating with her through his hand out of a desperate desire to have him here, awake with her, he squeezed again. This time she knew it had really happened. She saw it. She'd watched it, his index finger, flexing ever so slightly, but meaningfully, with intent.

As she waited for another sign from him, the slow, mournful picking of his guitar floated from the speaker she'd set up next to the flowers on the bedside table.

"I'm right here," she said.

His Adam's apple slid up and down on his neck like he was trying to swallow. Then his eyes opened a sliver and Elena felt her whole body rushing with warm water.

She scooted the chair over so that she could be nearer to his face.

As his eyes opened wider, she leaned over and smiled down at him.

He seemed not to recognize her at first. His eyes weren't quite focused. They gazed up, taking nothing in, as though his mind hadn't woken up yet. He manipulated his lips, kneading them against each other, trying to form words that wouldn't come.

It took all of his effort, but he finally managed to push out a hoarse sound. "Elena."

"Yes, Jake, I'm right here."

The corners of his lips turned almost imperceptibly upward and, breathing deeply for the first time in over a week, he let his eyes shut again.

"Where am I?" he said.

"You're at the hospital. You've been asleep."

He nodded without opening his eyes again.

For a long minute he remained still, breathing deeply, and Elena worried that he was sinking back into his coma, but finally, he said, "What happened?"

Elena's heart seized up inside her. She'd known she would have to answer this question if Jake ever woke up, but she hadn't thought she'd be confronted with it so soon. Straightening his hair with the flat of her hand, she asked him if he remembered anything.

"There was a buzzing." He breathed deeply. Talking exhausted him. "Like a bee."

Elena wanted to tell him the truth, she really did. Just not right now. Not as the first thing he heard. He'd hate her. And he'd be right to hate her. "You were stung," she said.

"How? I don't . . ." He huffed and paused to catch his breath. "I'm careful around bees. I'm . . . allergic."

Thankfully, he kept his eyes shut throughout this conversation. The thought that some tension in her face might betray her and tip him off to her guilt was too much for Elena to bear.

"I know," she said, soothing him, running her hand repeatedly through his hair. Nathaniel's threat burned at the front of her brain. "It . . . it must have slipped in through the window—or when you opened the door to get in. I don't know. A horrible accident. That's all I can think it was."

He opened his eyes again and gazed into hers. She could see the thankfulness and trust pouring out of him toward her and the tension in her chest twisted ever tighter until she felt the shame rise to her cheeks and she had to turn away.

Jake's music, which had been playing all this time, abruptly came to an end and the room suddenly filled with silence. This, somehow, more than anything else, pointed out to her how deeply she'd betrayed him. What kind of person had she turned into that she'd baldly lie like this to the boy she loved? She didn't deserve him. Not at all. But knowing this just made her need him that much more.

The tears began to stream down her cheeks.

Jake tried to raise his hand to wipe them away, but he could only mange to lift his hand six inches off the bed before it fell limply back to his side.

"What's wrong?" he asked.

She climbed into the bed and wrapped her leg across his torso, pressing herself into him, clinging to his chest. She was sobbing now. Her whole body shook.

"Elena," he said. "What's wrong?"

She kissed him on the collarbone above the loose neckline of his hospital gown.

"Nothing's wrong," she said. "I love you is all."

On the roof level of the visitor's lot at Sloan-Whitney Hospital, the black checkerboard Mini gleamed in the sun like someone had mounted it there in preparation for an ad. From a distance, it looked brand-new.

Squeezing Jake's hand, Elena said, "There it is." She smiled at him, shyly.

"Cameron had it brought up here, for when you recovered," said Jake's mother. She reached up and massaged his neck. "Like we knew you would," she added.

They'd all come to help him check out of the hospital—Elena, Jake's mom, Cameron.

The expression on Jake's face said it all. Wonderment. A wistful thankfulness at being alive. The world was a beautiful place and he was glad he was still in it. Even Cameron seemed more benign than before—Jake had watched how attentive and caring he'd been toward his mother over the past few days, canceling everything on his schedule in order to be there in the hospital with them, and he was thankful for this. He wasn't Dad—he could never replace Dad—but the man had a good heart.

Jake still couldn't speak above a whisper, but as they approached the car, he pushed out a hoarse thanks and said, "I'm surprised it survived."

Cameron ran a hand through his mane and winked at Jake. "Nothing but a tiny ding on the front fender," he said. "We had it taken care of. Look." He knelt next to the driver's-side wheel and ran his hand over the repaired fender. "Good as new."

Jake shook his head in wonder at his good fortune.

"You'd barely gotten out of your parking spot," Elena said. Since he'd been awake, she'd begun to explain things to him, filling in the gaps in his memory. "And the cars were backed up like they always are after school."

Jake squinted and smiled through his headache at her. The way she'd begun to intercede between him and the world, running interference, trying to cushion him from too much stimulation, was cute, endearing. What he couldn't understand was why, when he tried to reach out to her in moments like this, she flinched.

Like now: instead of meeting his eyes and making

one of her funny faces, she turned her head away, looked at the ground, and slid on her sunglasses.

"Relieved?" Cameron asked Jake, patting the car like it was a new pet.

"Yeah. But, uh, Dr. Lawrence said I can't drive until he clears me."

Cameron pressed the button on the key that unlocked the doors. "I'm driving today."

"Can we all even fit in there?" Elena said, peering in the window at the sliver of space that made up the backseat.

"I'm parked downstairs," Jake's mom said. "Cameron's going to drive Jake, and you and I will follow in the Lexus. We'll meet at the house, where there's muffins and pastries waiting for us courtesy of Tiki Tiki Java."

Jake frowned. "What about if Elena drove the Mini and Cameron rode with you, Mom?"

His mother and Cameron glanced at each other, sending messages back and forth for a moment.

"Sure," his mom said finally. She ruffled his hair like he was a child and then turned her attention to Elena. "Take care of this boy. He's fragile right now."

"I know," Elena said. "You can count on me. I'll protect him with my life."

Cameron lobbed the keys to her like he was shooting a basketball and then he and Jake's mom wandered arm in arm back toward the ramp leading down to the interior floors of the parking garage.

Settled in the passenger seat of the Mini, Jake watched as Elena adjusted the seat until it was pulled forward as far as it could go. She seemed uncomfortable, jittery. She kept glancing around like she was looking for an escape hatch. Maybe it was because she hated driving. Or maybe it was because of what had happened last time he'd been in the car.

"You'll do fine," Jake said. "This car is amazing. It almost drives itself."

He explained the various controls, the turn signal, the buttons that controlled the windows, the AC, and through it all, she couldn't even look in his direction. Every time she tried, her eyes gravitated to the passenger-seat floor. Maybe she was just spooked. Jake tried to ignore it. If he showed her he was strong, maybe his bravery would rub off on her.

"You ready?" Jake whispered. "Just turn the key."

She did as he said, her hand quivering, and navigated them down the looping pathway out of the garage. She stopped at the sign and then turned out onto Marine Drive.

"You okay?" asked Jake. "I've never seen you so quiet."

"Yeah, I'm . . . I'm fine." He could tell she was lying, but he didn't push it. His head still throbbed, deep under the surface. He could almost ignore it as long as he didn't try to think too hard. Sadly, talking her through whatever it was she was feeling was too much for him right now.

She turned onto Pleasant, heading toward Magnolia. Her hands were shaking and he could tell she was squeezing the steering wheel as tightly as she could to control them.

He had to do something to let her know he cared. "You don't seem fine," he said.

She stared straight ahead silently. Then she pounded the palm of her hand on the steering wheel.

"It's not fair," she said.

"What's not fair?" Jake asked.

She wouldn't look at him. With her sunglasses on, he couldn't gauge what was going on behind her eyes. "Nothing," she said. "It's my own fucking fault. I don't have a right to whine about it."

Now he really didn't know what she was talking about. Something having to do with Harlow? Some secret betrayal that she'd perpetrated while he was lying unconscious in his hospital bed? No. He told himself not to let his imagination run wild. He trusted her. He had no reason not to trust her. But then, what?

When he tried to comfort her with a hand on her knee, he could feel her muscles tense and recoil at his touch. He could feel himself beginning to become alarmed. His headache flashed like lightning across his forehead.

"Elena," he said. "Will you talk to me? Today's

supposed to be a good day. I survived. I'm going home. Just tell me what's wrong,"

They were stopped at a light. She whipped off her sunglasses and he could finally see her eyes—intense, defensive, clouded with self-loathing. "You really want to know?"

The words shot violently out of her mouth and he winced like she'd just slapped him.

"It was me," she said. "I put those bees in your car. I didn't *know* it was your car at the time, but that's no excuse. I still did it. That asshole Harlow convinced me that I had to protect him from some bullshit drug dealers who wanted him dead. It was stupid. But I believed him. And . . ." She'd run out of things to say. Well, except for one. "And I almost killed you."

And then she just stared at him like she was engulfed in some fire of her own making, like she was waiting for him to shove her into the street, to take the wheel and run her over.

For an instant, he felt the blood surging through his veins, pumping with great pressure against his brain, and he almost thought he might be capable of this violence.

But no. He wouldn't do that. Elena was as much of a victim as he was. No matter what she had done to inadvertently hurt him, he could never bring himself to cause her pain. Nathaniel, he was the one who deserved to be punished. Visions of the guy on his knees, begging for mercy, flashed through Jake's head. They embarrassed him. He didn't want to become the kind of person who took pleasure, like Nathaniel did, in others' pain. He just wanted to make sure Nathaniel could never hurt him or Elena again.

He calmly stared at her. It was time to contact Arnold.

The car behind them honked and Elena realized the light had changed. She hit the gas a touch too hard and they jolted through the intersection.

Jake just went on staring.

"Say something, Jake. Tell me you hate me."

"You mean Nathaniel," he said. "Not Harlow. Nathaniel."

"Exactly," she said. "Nathaniel. And you kept telling me that Harlow wasn't who he claimed to be and I didn't listen and then it turned out to be *him* and—wait, you knew it was Nathaniel? Why didn't you tell me?"

"I was going to. That day. Remember I said I had something to tell you? Arnold Chan and I put together some research. IP addresses. Screenshots and stuff."

He reached out and touched her knee. This time her muscles relaxed under his hand.

"It's okay," he said. "Elena, it's okay. I'm not mad at you."

"Well, we should do something," she blustered. "We should punish Nathaniel. We should—"

"No," said Jake. "No. Forget Nathaniel. He's not worth the effort."

"But—"

"Think about it. Here I am. Here you are. We're both still alive. And he did us a favor in a way. He brought us together. We should thank him for being such a douche bag, really."

Elena threw him a skeptical glance.

Chuckling, Jake said, "And also, Cameron told me this morning that he's transferred Nathaniel's trust fund into my name. Let him stew on that."

As they continued down the length of Magnolia Boulevard, Jake thought about the justice of the situation. The sun was shining. The palms were rustling in the breeze. Elena was here by his side. Nathaniel had lost everything, despite his tricks and mind games. Maybe it really was a beautiful day.

"What if he tries to come after you again?" she asked.

Jake tipped his head mischievously. "He won't."

"You can't be sure of that."

"Oh, but I am. You're just going to have to trust me on that."

It was time. Jake slipped his phone out of his pocket and pulled up Arnold's contact information. He typed a quick text: "READY, SET, GO!"

They continued on down Magnolia until they came to the intersection of Shore Drive. Elena hit the left turn blinker and waited for the green light.

The light didn't turn.

After a minute, the red warning hand was blinking in a weird way. Then the white walking figure flickered on, flickered off, and flickered on again.

"Something weird's happening," Elena said.

"Is it?" Jake said, trying to keep his poker face.

She peered at the stoplight. Now it had gone from red to yellow.

"Definitely," she said. "You seeing these lights?"

It wasn't just the stoplights. The lights in the stores up and down the street were flickering weirdly, too.

"Wait for it," Jake said. He counted out one, two, three with his fingers.

And all the lights went out at once.

"You know something about this?" she asked him.

"I wouldn't say that," he told her. "But if I had to guess, I'd say it looks like Nathaniel broke into the Dream Point power grid and sabotaged the computer system that controls the electricity. You know, hacking into a government agency is a federal crime. Two-hundred-fifty-thousand-dollar fine. Mandatory five years in jail."

Finally, he allowed himself to laugh.

Elena stared at him for a second, gauging how seriously to take what he'd just said. Then she laughed, too.

They laughed together.

SIMPLY JOY

First there's music *over a blank white screen. A quiet, tender strumming on an acoustic guitar.*

Then Jake's voice, strong and pure, no sign of damage. He sings of all the ways he's always known that Elena was the girl he loved. A simple song. Just a list.

The way she draws her life in exquisitely expressive pictures.

A line draws itself on the white background. It turns into Elena's face—not Electra's but Elena's, in a realistic mode.

Jake sings of Elena's toughness.

The face takes on a tough expression.

Her sensitivity.

The face changes, softens, smiles.

Her undying love for cookie-dough ice cream.

A carton of Ben & Jerry's floats in. Elena's body is drawn now and she holds the ice cream, spooning some into her mouth.

The constantly changing stickers she plasters all over her computer.

The ice cream carton morphs into a Mac and a barrage of anime stickers begin adhering to it, covering parts of each other up.

The way she bops her head, tipping it to the side, skeptical, flirtatious, a gleam in her eye.

The way she skips a step sometimes when she's walking along the sidewalk.

A sidewalk appears and Elena skips along it.

"The way she dances when she dances with me," sings Jake.

Jake—not Jaybird, but Jake—skips up alongside Elena. They dance in joyful circles, slowly rising off the ground as the lyrics fade away and are replaced by a simple but lyrical finger picking.

They float into the clouds, still dancing with each other.

"The way she completes me and makes my life worth living."

The finger picking continues.

Gradually, the black-and-white line drawings fill in

with color. First Elena and Jake. Then the clouds and the sky. Then finally, a rainbow arching over them, binding them in its beauty.

And still they dance.

EPILOGUE

Nathaniel sat on a beat-up aluminum bench wired to the chain-link fence in the dusty far corner of the yard. It was his usual spot, far enough from the Bloods playing basketball to avoid the run-ins he'd had with them in his first few weeks at Coleman Penitentiary but also too far out toward the wall—and the prying eyes constantly watching from the guard tower—to have to worry about the fiercer, and more dangerous Aryan Nation dudes pumping iron inside the workout cage.

Since arriving at the prison, he'd developed a number of survival strategies. He'd relied on his charm and aura of entitlement (and the perks he was able to get from the guards based on his graceful manners and ability to pay) to secure cigarettes and nudie mags and other contraband that he could then either sell or give away for favors and protection from the tougher, more physically intimidating guys who'd tried to make him their punk in his first few weeks. With a little help from Paco, the six-foot-six, 285-pound enforcer, known for his rippling bald head and the tattoo of a vulture spanning his entire back, Nathaniel had managed, pretty quickly, to gain control of the black market. By now, a year into his sentence, he and the gangs had developed a cautious understanding. He stayed out of their turf wars and they left him alone to run his shop.

Meanwhile, he'd gathered a gang of his own. Besides Paco, there was Willie Riggs, Little Jay, Lazy Eye, and Old Bobby McTeague. They ran his product to the various cell blocks for him and generally hung on his every word, basking in his reflected luster and imagining how different their lives would have been if they'd been given the leg up he'd had.

They called themselves the Smarts, not because they were all that intelligent, but because they'd all taken to wearing their prison blues in the tailored way Nathaniel did. None of that pants-around-the-knees stuff for them. They'd taken in the waists and rolled up the cuffs, tucking in their shirts so that, if not for their worn faces and oddly shaped bodies, they looked like they might have walked out of the pages of a special jailhouse-themed issue of *Vogue*.

Today they sat around him as usual, some lined up on either side of Nathaniel on the bench, some sitting on the ground. They smoked the Camels they reserved for themselves and made the most of the hour of fresh air they were allowed each day.

"You gonna miss us when you get out next week, Willie?" asked Lazy Eye, leaning forward on the bench and flashing his giant maniacal grin six inches from Willie's face. "I bet you are. I bet you're wishing you could shiv somebody and tack on another three years so you could hang around a little longer."

Willie, who never smiled, scowled at him. "Shee-it, man. Get out of my face before I knock your other eye loose." Pushing at Lazy Eye's chin, he shoved him away.

Paco and Old Bobby laughed at this, Old Bobby slapping his knobby hands together in laconic glee.

"You're getting out next week, Willie? You didn't tell me that." Nathaniel leaned back against the fence and tipped his head back so he look archly down his nose at Willie.

"It's true," said Willy, simply.

The rest of the gang glanced nervously at one another, unsure of whether Nathaniel was annoyed by the news or just tugging at the strings of his power like he sometimes did.

Nathaniel let Willie dangle for a moment.

Dragging long and hard off his cigarette, Willie stared back at him. None of these guys were the type to back down from a conflict.

"I'm going to have to find somebody to take over your beat on block C," said Nathaniel. "You've sort of screwed me here."

"See, that's why I didn't tell you. I didn't want to let you down, Boss."

Nathaniel smirked and stared across the yard at the basketball game in progress. He watched as a scrawny guy, just a kid really, new to the prison, went for a cross-over and was shoved to his back by the steel mountain that was Junior Suarez, the biggest, baddest guy on the court.

He could feel the guys waiting for him to give them something, a barrage of fancy words dressing Willy down, or a sly joke at his expense.

"It's cool," he said. "There's always new blood show-ing up in this place. I'll find somebody."

"Just say the word, Nate. I'll give them no choice," said Paco, bouncing his pecs to prove his worthiness.

Nathaniel smirked again. "But, Willy," he said, "you're not getting rid of me that easily. I've treated you pretty well in here, but the real prize is out there." He surveyed the faces of his disciples. "All of you, listen. I've got a proposal for you. Imagine, if you will, a hoary, aging hippie chick, maybe forty-five, fifty, getting too old to float through the scene at the beach any longer and now scared that she's going to die poor and alone. She owns a little run-down café that she can barely afford to keep open. And she's got a teenaged son, a tall, skinny guy who's so self-pitying that all he ever does is sit in the dark of his room and whine into his guitar.

"Now imagine a suave and cosmopolitan man, a playboy who owns half the world and toys with the other half. This man's wife died, tragically, a number of years ago and he's been very lonely for a long time now. He meets the woman. It doesn't matter how or where. What matters is that this woman, seeing him, casts a spell on him. She's learned some tricks during her years in the sandalwood-scented haze of the beach. She tricks him into falling in love with her.

"And before you know it, she's taken over his life. She's moved into his luxurious house on the beach. She's convinced him that everything he ever cherished before should be forsaken and replaced by her and her son.

"Now, the man has a son of his own, whom he'd worked hard to protect and provide for. But under the woman's spell, he takes everything he'd once promised his son and gives it all to hers, leaving his son nearly penniless, alone, struggling to survive."

He looked from face to face, meaningfully locking eyes with each guy one by one.

"Do you think that's right?"

"Naw, it ain't right at all," said Little Jay.

"Damn straight," Willie said.

Nathaniel nodded his agreement with their assessment. "See, that's where you all come in. You in particular, Willie. That suave, cosmopolitan playboy is my father. And the hippie woman, she's my stepmother. She stole my life from me. I want it back. And you, Willie, can help me now that you're getting out. I'll make it worth your while. This goes for all of you. What do you say?"

He could see the greed flushing their faces.

"I've got it all worked out," he said. "It's all I've been thinking about since I got locked up in here. The key is the son. Jake is his name. And the way to get to him is through his girlfriend, Elena. Now, here's what you have to do . . ."

Don't miss a moment of the
LIES, PASSION, and BETRAYAL
in the steamy beach town
of Dream Point . . .